"IT'S GONNA BE YOU AND ME AGAINST TWENTY MEN,"

said Concho crouching in the darkness, "and the first one that lets the other down, he's signin' both our death warrants."

He snapped a match and looked at Ramsey across the flame.

"Now, somebody got to be in charge of an operation like this. Let's get this settled. Who it gonna be, you or me?"

Ramsey looked at him a moment. Then he said, "I reckon it'll be you. This is more in your line."

Concho looked faintly surprised. "I jest wanted to have it understood. I mean, you a white man and . . . and I black."

Ramsey spat into the dust. "You're the expert," he said quietly. "Call the turn and I'll follow orders."

They stayed hidden in the arroyo for a long time—then made their move.

Other SIGNET Westerns
You Will Want to Read

BIG
BEND

BY RICHARD MEADE

A SIGNET BOOK from
NEW AMERICAN LIBRARY
TIMES MIRROR

SIGNET TRADEMARK REG. U.S. PAT. OFF. AND FOREIGN COUNTRIES
REGISTERED TRADEMARK—MARCA REGISTRADA
HECHO EN CHICAGO, U.S.A.

*SIGNET BOOKS are published by
The New American Library, Inc.,
1301 Avenue of the Americas, New York, New York 10019*

FIRST PRINTING, JANUARY, 1970

PRINTED IN THE UNITED STATES OF AMERICA

For Jim Henderson and
Monty Wilson

AUTHOR'S NOTE

With the exception of Rodolfo Fierro, Villa and the other prominent historical figures referred to, and the casually mentioned bandit Chico Cana, all characters in this novel are fictitious. So is the town of North Wells.

In 1914, Pancho Villa was, indeed, walking on eggs in his treatment of Americans, although later, to embarrass his opposition, he executed a number of American civilians and carried out the famous raid on Columbus, New Mexico, which resulted in the Army's punitive expedition led by General Pershing.

Villa also was one of the earliest military leaders to recognize the desirability of his own air force, and did possess one.

Today, the scene of this novel is the wildest and least-visited of all American National Parks.

BIG
BEND

⋆ CHAPTER ONE ⋆

Ramsey came over the hill and saw ahead of him the ranch house and the men waiting there. Five of them, they had hitched their horses and were lounging under the brush-covered *ramada* of the adobe ranch house. Ramsey put the bay Morgan gelding into a high lope. His big body seemed to overbalance the small horse, but, really, the Morgan, blood lines flawless and its muscles like spring steel, carried him easily.

As they saw Ramsey coming, the lounging men straightened up and faced him. Now he could see that they wore sidearms and that there were carbines in scabbards on their saddles. This was unusual in the Texas highlands of 1914, and Ramsey's shaggy brows went up in surprise.

When he reined in the Morgan in the ranch yard, it stopped on a dime, and Ramsey swung down. Even on the ground, he seemed to dwarf the little horse, for he was a great bear of a man in his mid-thirties, standing six feet and weighing well over two hundred. Beneath a shock of raven-black hair, his tanned face was not without humor, but just now his black eyes were guarded and neutral. He wore range clothes; battered Stetson, workshirt, scarred bullhide chaps over faded Levis, and high-heeled, bench-made boots which were without spurs, for no Ramsey-broken horse ever needed the touch of them.

"Tom," he said, dropping the Morgan's reins. "Jim; Al; howdy, Joe-Bob; Ralph, how you doing?" He held out a big, calloused hand and shook hands all around.

Tom Denning was, of course, spokesman for the group. He was in his early sixties, but it was said of him that he was still tough as rawhide and mean as a snake. The Denning ranch was the largest in the county, and Denning was a power in the Texas and Southwestern Cattle Raiser's Association.

"Hello, Ramsey," he said in a harsh, dry voice. His face was long and dour, his white mustache in startling contrast to its hue of sun-bronzed leather. He wore a collarless shirt, the best to an old suit, and a pair of ancient shotgun chaps. "We been waitin' a long time for you."

Ramsey shrugged. "Shoulda let me know you were comin'. What brings y'all down to this neck of the woods, all loaded for bear?"

"Not for bear," Denning said. "For rustlers."

Sam Ramsey stared at him for a moment. Then he said, "There's some beer in the house. Y'all come in and tell me what's up."

The front room of the ranch house was a man's place, spartanly furnished, clean as a pin, a good many books in shelves on the wall and a lot of horse-breeding journals and papers stacked beneath them. There were not enough chairs, and some of the men sat on Ramsey's bed, while he went into the kitchen and got six bottles of beer from the food safe. Opening them, he passed them around and squatted down with his back against the wall. The beer tasted wonderful after a day on the range.

After a long swig, Ramsey drew the back of a hairy hand across his mouth. "Okay, gentlemen, what's up?"

"I lost twenty-five head of stock this week," Denning said thinly. "That's what's up. We've had all we're gonna stand for, Ramsey. Shan Williams has deputized us all, and we're gonna put a stop to this cattle-liftin'. We know these rustlers work out of the deep part of the Big Bend country. Well, we've each sent three of our best men on down to Saul's place, and we'll jump off from there. We're takin' plenty of supplies and ammunition and we're not comin' back 'til we've rubbed out every cow-stealer down in those badlands. We want you to come along."

Ramsey halted the beer bottle in its upward journey to his mouth. "Kind of short notice," he said.

"We didn't decide we needed you 'til this mornin'. But that's bad country for horses down there, and you're a wonder with 'em. You'll be packmaster and in charge of stock."

Ramsey slid up the wall until he was on his feet, carefully keeping his temper reined in. That was typical of Denning; the old bastard thought all he had to do was snap his fingers, and everybody in the county would come running.

"Tom," Sam Ramsey said quietly, "I'd like to accommodate you. But I can't just drop everything and take off down into the desert on a wild-goose chase at a minute's notice. I run a one-man operation here—"

"Yeah, we know that." Denning's voice was impatient. "I'll send a couple of hands over to take care of things while you're gone."

"It ain't that easy. I got eight geldin's in the process of bein' broke. A couple of fumble-thumbed cowhands that think you buck a horse out and it's fit to ride, could ruin

10

ever' one of 'em." He took a swallow of beer, and now his voice was firm. "Nope, gentlemen, sorry. But I can't do it."

Denning stood up. "I won't take that kind of answer, Ramsey."

"It's the only one I can give you."

Denning's mouth thinned. "I don't think you understand the situation exactly. I don't think—"

"I understand the situation." Ramsey was not good with words, but he was beginning to get angry now, and he spoke quickly. "I understand it fine. You folks have been losing stock. Ten head here, twenty there. I know it hurts—"

"You damn well told it does!" Jim Harrigan put in. "You know what a cow-critter's worth now? Especially with this war in Europe?"

"I may be a horse rancher, but I know," Ramsey said. "I know somethin' else, too. I know you and your army can't go down in the deep Big Bend and even come within smellin' distance of whoever's doin' this rustlin'."

"What makes you so sure?" Denning challenged, eyes furious. "You ever been down there?"

"No," Ramsey said. "But I know what it's like. That's the wildest country left in Texas. Nothing but a few scattered shirttail ranches, a bunch of abandoned mines, dry creeks and water holes, and the damnedest badlands in the world. I don't know how many of them rustlers there are, but a thousand men could lose themselves down in there and you'd never git close to 'em. Even if you did, it ain't but a jump across the Rio Grande."

"If we have to, we'll cross the Rio after 'em!"

"And that's when you *will* git your tail in a crack! The other side of the Rio's just swarmin' with Mescan rebels and bandits. You invade their territory, they'll rub you and your boys out quicker'n you can spit. Tom, it's a job for the Army or the Rangers—"

"The Army!" Denning gave a hoarse laugh. "The Army says it ain't authorized to chase cattle-rustlers. And the Rangers are already tied up. They've pulled every man outa this area to go after Chico Cana, that Mexican bandit operatin' near Presidio."

"Maybe this is Cana, too, that's liftin' your stock."

"No, it ain't. He operates farther west; this is another gang entirely. Now, I'm givin' you one last chance, Ramsey. You comin' with us?"

Ramsey looked at him steadily and shook his head. "No. I ain't. I done told you that I can't afford to leave my horses for even two days, much less two weeks. Especially when you give me no notice at all . . . You better count me out."

11

There was a long silence in the room then, and Ramsey was perfectly aware of the resentment and hostility that charged the air as the five cattlemen, old-timers all, rich and powerful, looked at him.

Then Denning said, heavily, "All right, Ramsey. I reckon we ought to of expected it. These fence-cutters and cow-thieves ain't bothered with horses yet, so you figure it ain't your fight." His mustache fluttered as he let out a long breath. "The other boys told me you wouldn't come, but I thought I knowed better."

"What you mean is, you thought I wouldn't dare turn Tom Denning down."

Before Denning could answer, Jim Harrigan stood up. "Listen, Ramsey. We know you don't love us and we got no particular love for you. But this is a community effort—somethin' to benefit us all, you as much as the rest of us. That's why Tom figured you'd come. But we knowed you wouldn't. You don't give a damn for anybody in North Wells but yourself."

Ramsey said, in a carefully controlled voice, "Jim, you've been around here for a long time. You ever remember the time when North Wells gave a damn for the Ramseys?" He felt a savage pleasure in the way Harrigan's eyes shifted. Then his tone changed. "Why don't you put the same time and men into patrolling your fences—?"

"We don't need advice from you!" Denning's face was turkey-red. "We've all of us handled rustlers before, in the old days—!"

"These ain't the old days," Ramsey said evenly.

"Those cow-stealers down in Big Bend will think they are when we swing some of 'em," Denning said fiercely. Then he said, "All right, Ramsey, you made your bed, now lay in it. When you need some help, don't come cryin' to *us* for it."

Ramsey drew himself up straight. "You ever see me come cryin' to *anybody* for help?"

Denning didn't answer that. His gray eyes locked with Ramsey's for a moment; then he turned on his heel. "Come on, men," he growled. "We've wasted a lot of time and we got a long way to ride."

★   ★   ★

Sam Ramsey stood where he was as the five stalked out and mounted up. Hoofbeats pounded, in a quick, almost angry tempo. Then they faded, and slowly Ramsey went outside. Dust hung low over the six-mile lane to the main road, but the riders themselves were out of sight. The Morgan stood patiently, ground-reined, not having moved six inches.

Ramsey led the animal to a corral that contained three other horses, unsaddled it, wiped it down with a gunny sack, and turned it loose to drink and roll. Leaning on a fence post, he watched the animal flop down, try twice, then go over on the third roll, grunting with the ecstasy of it. But Ramsey was not thinking of the horse.

Maybe not joining the posse had been a mistake. That might have been the one gesture that would have healed all the old wounds, finally bridged the gap between himself and the town. But Denning had thrown it at him too fast; there'd been no time to think; and his first reaction had been to draw back, as he always did. Yes, there was no doubt that it was a mistake, even though going would have jeopardized the work of three months . . .

The sun slanted low, gilding the sides of hills, buttes, and mesas, painting purple shadows in draws and hollows, touching the sea of good grass with gold.

He could understand the way Denning felt. Revolution flamed and guttered on the other side of the Rio Grande. First, Madero against Diaz, then Huerta against Madero, and now Carranza and the famed Pancho Villa against Huerta. Almost four years of constant warfare, with Villa dominating, always up to his ears in revolution and counterrevolution alike. And now the northern border of Mexico had been picked clean, and the armies and bandit gangs and combinations of both that roved Chihuahua and Coahuila would pay dearly for gringo beef—and, Ramsey thought grimly, gringo horses.

So rustling had become worth the risk again. In Texas, the land had filled up and the cattlemen were strongly organized, and selling stolen beef north of the Rio had become so dangerous that cow-thieves were almost something out of the past. But they could not resist the safe and lucrative markets the armies below the Rio provided, and Southwest Texas was beginning to feel the effects of the waves of violence that lapped northward. There was no doubt that Denning and the others were hurting. A fat whiteface on the hoof was about the equivalent of a poke of gold.

Still, he doubted that they could flush the thieves out of the deep Big Bend. Down there, at the southernmost point of the great loop of the Rio Grande that gave the country its name, there were thousands of square miles of uninhabited desert, stark mountain ranges, some never totally explored, and probably not fifty honest inhabitants in the whole huge region. Denning was undoubtedly right—that was where the stolen

13

cattle were going. But finding a gang of twenty or thirty throwbacks to the old wild days down there was a different matter—especially since they could jump the border at the first sign of pursuit . . . Still, Denning was a veteran of the old days himself; if anybody could do it, he could.

The light had faded now, and Ramsey went back into the house. In the tiny kitchen, he cooked bacon and heated refried beans and opened another can of beer and sat down to his solitary meal. He was still nagged by his decision not to go.

And yet, he'd had no alternative. He raised Morgans here, the best, and trained them himself into the finest cow and cutting horses. It was a small operation, but a profitable one, and he didn't dare leave it for more than a day at a time. Not even Denning's offer to send men to run it while he was gone changed that. Nobody handled horses the way he did, and in two weeks ignorant men could ruin them all.

Finishing his meal, he washed up and stowed everything as carefully as any old maid. Then he stripped and took a quick shower under a homemade rig outdoors beside the windmill. Putting on clean underwear, he set the alarm clock, got into bed, read by the light of a kerosene lamp for a half hour, blew out the lamp, and went quickly to sleep. Not long before midnight, the clock awakened him. He arose, splashed water on his face, drank two cups of strong coffee, and dressed.

After he'd buckled his chaps, he took a gun belt from the wall and strapped it on. In the holster was a .45 Colt single-action inherited from his father. The .30-.30 Winchester and its soft, well-oiled scabbard that he carried outside was also a legacy.

There was no need to use a rope to saddle a fresh horse; every mount in the corral was trained to come at a whistle and to stand motionless while it accepted the bit.

Then minutes later, he rode at a high lope away from the home ranch toward the pasture that held his breeding stock. The moon was full and high, its light turning ridge and butte and grassland to silver, a sight to make a man catch his breath. At this altitude the wind was cool, even on a summer night, and Ramsey's heavy jacket felt good.

Another twenty minutes, and fifteen Morgan mares raised their heads and pricked their ears as he came into sight. One old mare and Dancing Man, his fine stallion, took a few wary steps toward him until they caught his scent and relaxed. He rode on around them, opened and closed a gate; and then he was in the pasture with his thirty-two young three- and four-year-old geldings, most of which were already receiving training of some kind. Grazing among them were the twenty head

14

of wild Mexican steers he kept, not for beef but for training purposes. At the sight of a mounted man, most of them spooked and lumbered off, tails high.

Everything was in order. Sam Ramsey relaxed, bent a thick, muscular leg around the saddle horn, and, full of pride and satisfaction, smoked a cigarette. From now until almost dawn, he would keep watch over his horses.

He had been doing this ever since the rustling started. It was a grueling schedule for a man alone, but the idea of hiring anyone to help him had never even occurred to Sam Ramsey. Besides, as he would not trust Denning's men with his Morgans, neither would he trust any pickup cowhand.

Not that he really expected trouble. His ranch was small, its southern border protected by the range of Jim Harrigan's huge Lazy H that adjoined it. The cattle of the big ranchers, whose spreads extended south for miles, were far easier and more tempting pickings Still, he would take no chances. For his horses were his life's work and all he had in the world.

That thought filled him with a strange restlessness. It was something that had bothered him more and more of late, something mixed up with the frequent, overwhelming desire that occasional bouts with the Mexican girls in North Wells no longer totally relieved. It had taken him a while to search out its cause, but at last he'd figured it out. He was getting on into his thirties and it was time he got himself a woman, somebody with whom to share what he had built up and who would bear him some children to pass it all along to. It surprised him how urgent that need in him had become.

But what woman would want him? More important, what woman did he want? Sure, there was a handful of eligible girls in North Wells, but the thought of living with any one of them filled him with a kind of nausea. Not a one of them, anyhow, who wouldn't consider him beneath her, and probably not a one whose family he wouldn't have to fight to get. The people of North Wells had a long memory; no one knew that better than Sam Ramsey. For forty years, over an ancient grudge, they had made outcasts of his parents, and even now that both of them were buried, it was something that neither he nor the town had yet forgotten.

So the hell with them, he thought. He was used to being alone, and he could stand it for a long time. But when he no longer could, then he would get himself a woman—but not from North Wells. Meanwhile, he'd go on as he had for years, shying clear of getting mixed up with others, depending on no one but himself . . .

He slipped his right foot back into the stirrup, reined his mount around, and began to ride the rest of his fence, straight in the saddle, alert and watchful. But there was nothing but the occasional soundless flight of an owl and the distant, shrill yip of a coyote. At the end of a four-hour hitch, when it would be too late for thieves to strike and get away before daylight, he turned homeward, where he went to bed again and slept until just after seven.

★ CHAPTER TWO ★

Ten days later, it happened that Sam Ramsey was in town when Denning's expedition returned.

North Wells had a railroad spur and a population of a thousand people, sixty percent of them Mexican. Its scattered buildings baked on a shadeless flat, and even though its unpaved main street had been oiled, each fresh breeze still roiled dust and coated everything with a fine, yellow powder.

Ramsey had bought supplies at Finney's Mercantile and was loading them in a wagon when he saw the column coming. They were still a long way off, outside of town, moving at a walk, as if their horses were exhausted; the shimmer of heat at that distance blurred all other details.

There was more still to be loaded, but instead of returning to the store, Ramsey shoved a pile of salt blocks into place and wiped his hands against his jeans. Then he leaned on the wagon and waited, squinting into the sun.

Slowly the men drew nearer—about twenty of them and some led horses. Now the column reached the head of Main Street, and Ramsey could see Tom Denning in its lead, his white mustache so dusty that it was barely visible against his burnt-black face.

Word got around fast in North Wells; the board sidewalks were crowded, excited onlookers raising a hum like bees. As Denning and his men rode down the street, people surged forward to meet them. But Ramsey stood where he was, counting men and horses. Then he made a small sound in his throat. He knew that twenty had ridden out, but the column now was made up of only eighteen men.

Long before they reached Ramsey, the riders swung over to the side of the street and halted before The Texas Cattleman, largest of the town's saloons. They swung down, and the crowd boiled around them. Ramsey saw Denning snap something at them ferociously, tie his mount, and shove

16

through the throng. The others followed, their faces dust-covered and gaunt, their eyes hollow.

As Sam Ramsey himself walked toward the saloon, Sheriff Shan Williams emerged from the adobe building that was his office. A lanky man in Stetson, boots, and a seersucker suit, a Colt automatic strapped around his waist, he stood blinking in the sunlight and then hastened across the street and vanished into the barroom.

By the time Ramsey got there, the crowd blocked him off from the men at the bar. Tom Denning, holding a glass of cold beer, was talking to Sheriff Williams in a voice loud enough for everyone to hear.

"They wouldn't even try to fight. They knew every back trail and draw in the whole damned place. They jest kept fadin' out in front of us all the way to the Rio, and then they crossed. We went after 'em, and that's where we got into the fight and Lee and Buck got killed. We crossed at San Vicente and we wasn't two miles into Coahuila before the Mescans hit us. A whole damn army of 'em, Villa's men, I reckon. Anyhow, they had us five to one, and we had a hell of a fight to git back across the river, and we had to leave Lee and Buck behind. They didn't chase us across the Rio—"

"So you never found the cow-thieves," Shan Williams said.

Denning took a swig of beer. "No. Not the main bunch of 'em. I told you, they just sifted out ahead of us. That country down there, it's a nightmare. You got the Chisos and the Dead Horse Mountains and the del Carmens in Mexico, and when it ain't up, it's straight down, and when it ain't either one, it's miles of mean desert. Maybe if it hadn't been for the Mescans, we might of finally made 'em stand and fight. But when you got the protection of a whole damn regiment of Mex *Revolucionarios*, you don't need to fight." He slammed his hand on the bar. "It's a job for the Army, that's what we've found out. The only way to clean out that country is for the Army to git up off its ass and move in." He finished the beer. "Take at least a regiment of cavalry."

"The Army won't move, you know that," Williams said. "They got less than fifteen hundred men at Fort Bliss, most of 'em infantry. They say it's my responsibility as the civilian law. Maybe I should have gone along—"

"It wouldn't have done a bit of good," Denning snapped. "We got whipped, and we got whipped good, and it wouldn't have made a bit of difference whether you or the Angel Gabriel or anybody else was along. What we got to do now is apply pressure on Washington, make that damned college professor up there send the soldiers out—"

Williams nodded. "Well, maybe you're right." He turned to

17

a tall, wide-shouldered man next to Denning, a man who had the look of being made of rawhide and whipcord. "Billy, I'm sorry about Lee."

Billy Goodhue's face was something like that of a frog, his eyes haunted. The wide mouth thinned. "Thanks, Shan," he mumbled and turned away. This was Denning's foreman; his brother had been one of those left in Mexico.

Williams turned to face the crowd. "Now, you people break it up. These men have had all they need without you folks botherin' 'em. Shoo! Scat!" He flapped his hands at them like a man chasing flies.

Slowly and reluctantly, the crowd flowed to the door. Ramsey stood to one side and let it pass. Soon the place was nearly empty; even the sheriff had gone. A little uncertainly, Ramsey moved up to the bar and touched Tom Denning on the shoulder.

Denning whirled nervously, and Billy Goodhue looked around.

"Tom," Ramsey said, "I'm sorry as hell."

Denning stared at him, eyes pale in the tanned, dusty face. Then he said, "Yeah. I bet you are. All right, go ahead, say it. You told us so."

"I ain't going to say anything. I just—"

"Then don't say anything!" Billy Goodhue rapped. He straightened up, as tall as Ramsey, and his voice was like flint against flint. "Anybody too chicken-livered to come with us—"

Ramsey felt his face burn. He took a step backwards. "Billy," he said quietly, "you're dog-tired and sufferin' a loss. I'll overlook what you said. And . . . I'm sorry about Lee."

"Lee don't need your sorry. He mighta used your gun when we was in that fight across the river." Goodhue's eyes were like coals in his face.

"I had my reasons for not going—"

"Yeah. Sure." Goodhue's weary frog-mouth twisted, and he turned back to the bar. "Ahhh," he said contemptuously. "Bastards like you make me sick."

He had used a word that was, in South Texas at that time, unforgivable. All at once, the room was silent, except for the scrape of boots and the rustle of chaps, as the other men at the bar turned. Ramsey, aware of all those eyes on him, stood motionless, staring at Goodhue's broad back, his face flaming.

"Billy," he said, "I'm sorry you got whipped and lost your brother. But don't take it out on me."

Without even looking around, Goodhue said something contemptuous and obscene. The others drew in their breaths.

18

They were expecting him to jump Goodhue now, Ramsey knew. It was what the man wanted—an opponent he could get his hands on, somebody he could fight, not an elusive shadow or a whole army, but just another man, a big one, a strong one, so he could vent his grief and frustration. It had been a mistake to speak, Ramsey realized. But then, it always was a mistake to get mixed up with the people of North Wells.

But he did not want to fight Goodhue, and he didn't care, really, what others thought of him. Anyhow, Goodhue was drunk with fatigue, and a sober man didn't fight drunks. Ramsey fought himself under control, wordlessly turned away, and took a step toward the door.

Goodhue whirled and caught him, thick fingers gouging his arm. Goodhue's face was contorted. "You yellow coward. You won't fight even when somebody rubs your nose in it, will you?"

"Billy," Denning said in a cautionary voice.

Ramsey looked into eyes that were feverish with a temporary insanity. When he said, evenly, "Billy, turn me loose," Goodhue did not seem to hear.

Then, roughly, he shoved Ramsey away. "Yankee skunk," he said.

And that was enough. Ramsey felt the control and compassion rush out of him; hot, red rage enter in. His fists clenched, his voice shook. "All right, Billy, you wanted it, you got it. Take off that goddam gun and we'll go outside."

A slow, triumphant grin overspread Goodhue's face. "Well, by God," he said, and his hand unlatched his cartridge belt. He handed it to Denning, without taking his eyes from Ramsey. "Hold that a minute, boss."

Ramsey wheeled, strode out the door into the hot, bright sunlight. He heard Goodhue's boots clomping behind him, eagerly, the rush as the others followed. He stepped down off the sidewalk and into the middle of the oiled street, and then he turned to face Goodhue, who was coming at him fast.

There were no preliminaries. Goodhue came off the sidewalk at a run, big fists clubbed, and Ramsey met him head-on. Neither man had any knowledge of boxing; both were work-hardened and tough; they moved in close and began to batter each other with short, powerful jabs. Goodhue's beardy, dusty face danced before Sam Ramsey's eyes; and Ramsey felt the shock and pain as Goodhue's heavy fists clubbed him on shoulders, arms, and chest. But he was dealing out the same punishment to Goodhue, each looking for a chance to

19

smash the other's face, neither with room enough in which to do it.

Then Ramsey stepped back, got leeway, and before Goodhue could close with him again, he hit Goodhue on the mouth hard enough to rock him back. Then Ramsey followed up with a left that knocked Goodhue's face around. Goodhue lurched to one side, knees buckling, but he caught Ramsey around the waist as he dropped and buried his face in Ramsey's shirt. Ramsey hit him on the back of the neck, but Goodhue slid down, seized Ramsey's legs, up-ended him, and Ramsey fell backwards on the street with terrific impact. He was scrambling up when Goodhue, laughing and bleeding, hit him between the eyes and knocked him flat again.

Stars exploded and lights went off in Ramsey's head. Then he felt a crushing, smothering weight on him—Goodhue. Fingers gouged into the soft flesh of his throat, looking for the windpipe. Ramsey, knowing that he was dead unless he broke that grip, threshed his body desperately, somehow got a hand in Goodhue's face. His fingers sought the eyes, as he pushed Goodhue's head backwards with all his power.

Then Goodhue had to yield or break his neck. His fingers nearly tore out Ramsey's throat as they slipped away. Suddenly Goodhue's weight was off him, and Ramsey was rolling frantically, knowing that the first one up had the advantage. He made it to his feet a fraction of a second before Goodhue, while the cowboy was still off balance, and hit Goodhue in the face with all the force of right fist, arm, and shoulder. Goodhue sagged sideways, landed on hands and knees in the dust, blood pouring from nose and mouth. He shook his head and tried to hoist himself; to make sure he didn't, Ramsey hit him again, and Goodhue flopped over on his back, arms and legs spraddled, mouth open, breath a rasp.

Ramsey stood tensely, fists clubbed, waiting for Goodhue to rise, then saw that it was over. He sucked in a gulp of air that made his chest swell and spat into the dust from a dry mouth. Brushing hair back from his eyes, he wheeled to face Tom Denning.

"All right, Ramsey," Denning said coldly. "You won't hafta fight nobody else."

"Billy asked for it— He wouldn't let me out of it . . ."

"Yeah, he overstepped. It was fair." But there was no warmth or friendliness in the words, and Ramsey, looking at the hostile faces that ringed him, knew that every man there regretted his victory. He was alone in the town, as always. But he had showed them that it made no difference. Still gasping, he turned away, shoved through the crowd, and walked stiffly and painfully to his wagon outside Finney's Mercantile.

★　　★　　★

He still felt the effects of the fight that night as he rode his fences. Billy Goodhue had landed plenty of solid blows, and even the Morgan's rocking-chair gait made Ramsey wince. By an hour after midnight, he was already looking forward to dawn and time to head back to the house. It was too bad, he thought, that he lacked corral space to keep the whole herd near the ranch house at night.

Because of the ugliness of the afternoon, his thoughts tonight were sour and pessimistic. The wind seemed colder than usual, and he was acutely aware of his loneliness. Maybe he did need a woman, maybe—

Then, not far away in the other pasture, the stallion, Dancing Man, snorted.

Ramsey reined around, hand dropping to the cedar butt of the old .45.

Horses have a language; Ramsey knew and understood it. Dancing Man wasn't clearing his nostrils or warning a colt away from his graze. He had caught the wind of something strange, alarming. Probably only a coyote or a bobcat, but, still—

The moon was high, a suspended blob of hammered silver. Its light made shadows extravagant, tricky. Ramsey looked at the geldings in this pasture; most of them still grazed or slept, but a few had lifted their heads and pricked their ears. Then Dancing Man snorted again. At that moment, a swirl of cloud veiled the moon and shrouded the earth with darkness.

Ramsey cursed silently and drew the .45. The pressure of his knee sent the Morgan at a cautious walk toward the gate between the pastures, a few hundred yards away. Suddenly, heart pounding, he reined in. The wind had risen and it blew away from him; then it died for an instant and he heard the sound again, almost certainly a voice. A word or two, indistinguishable, then the wind once more.

Now the thunder of hooves; the brood mares had spooked, were galloping about the pasture. Ramsey put the Morgan into a lope, straining his eyes to pierce the darkness ahead. The sound of running horses ahead of him drowned out its hoofbeats. Suddenly the animal slid to a stop; it had reached the gate.

Then, from beyond it, there was a high, strange scream, a sound to freeze the blood. Ramsey recognized it, a cry of rage from a charging stallion; it came again, and suddenly

21

there was the explosion of gunfire, a lacing of bright flashes in the night. The horse screamed again, this time in agony, and Ramsey reached frantically for the wire loop that held the homemade gate. His hand had just touched it when he was blinded by a white, glaring light. Instinctively, he fired full at it, and it fell to the ground, a carbide lantern raying upward now. In its beam he saw the man he had caught by surprise at the gate crumpling to one knee, his led horse jerking free behind him and racing off down the fence. Ramsey shot again and the man flopped over on his back, and then the gate sagged open and Ramsey kicked the Morgan through. A final scream from Dancing Man was chopped off short. Ramsey raced the horse down the fence toward gun flashes, firing as he went at those bright orange jets, drawing down their lightning on himself.

It came: a deadly, winking flicker of orange and the raw and ripping whine of near-miss bullets. His hammer clicked down on an empty shell; he clawed at the Winchester. Then the Morgan shuddered, grunted, reared and fell sideways. Ramsey was almost thrown from the saddle, but not quite; the horse came down as dead weight against the fence, and Ramsey was still mounted on it. Barbed strands gouged his flesh; fence posts snapped; wire rolled over and around him and, as the horse landed hard on his left leg, Ramsey's head hit something and seemed to explode in a flash of brilliant white light. After that, there was only darkness.

⋆ CHAPTER THREE ⋆

Wrapped in a cocoon of jumbled wire, Sam Ramsey awakened to scalding sunlight and to pain. His head felt as if it were about to split like a rotten melon; his wire-chewed torso was stiff with dried blood and ached in every muscle—and his left leg was numb from the thigh down, pinned beneath the dead Morgan's rib cage.

Ramsey thought, when he could think at all: It's full day; they can't still be around. And they haven't killed me . . . Slowly, cautiously, panting as he disentangled himself from the wire, he raised himself on one elbow and craned his neck. That much effort made his head roar with pain, his eyes water. But there was no one within the radius of his vision: Both pastures were empty, as far as he could see.

22

He sank back, waited for the blade of pain in his skull to quit sawing, and tried to think.

For the moment, the most important thing was to get out from under the dead horse. If he didn't, he would die slowly and in agony, for no one from North Wells would ever come looking for him. He dug his elbows into the ground and pulled.

But the Morgan weighed nearly half a ton, and its full weight was on him; moreover, his foot seemed tangled in the stirrup. The animal's carcass held him like the jaws of a trap.

He pulled his right leg up, braced his foot against the saddle, and tried harder, hoping his boot would come off. But that didn't work, either.

Ramsey sank back, panting, exhausted. Above him, the high, blue bowl of the sky turned to brass as the sun climbed to zenith. Against the limitless space, black flakes swirled and circled—vultures.

Presently, he regained strength and tried again. He fought the dead horse, pushed, pulled, shoved at it savagely, desperately. But as if, in death, it bore a grudge, it would not let him go. Now Ramsey was more afraid than sick. Even if he didn't die here, a few more hours and gangrene in that pinned leg was a certainty. It seemed impossible that he could die—of thirst, dehydration, starvation—not a mile from his own house; but unless he worked that leg free, it would not be impossible at all.

If he yielded to panic, all was lost. Breathing hard, fighting back fear and frustration that made him want to scream, he grasped the saddle horn and pulled himself into an awkward sitting position. Craning his head, he looked around as far as he could.

The grass of the empty pastures rippled under a slight breeze. The horse had fallen not far from the wire gate, and the gate itself was wide open. To one side of it lay the body of the first man he had ever killed, face up.

Ramsey twisted farther around, straining every muscle. Then he tensed. Far out in the brood-mare pasture, there was a solitary dot, mouse-gray against the golden grass.

Hope rose in Ramsey, but he fought it down. It could be one of the Mexican cattle, with which he worked his horses. Or it could be one of the young geldings that had wandered into the other pasture—maybe one too young to be fully trained. But there was a chance that the raiders had missed a full-grown brood mare in the darkness, and if that were the case . . .

Ramsey licked dried and cracked lips. He sucked in a deep

23

breath, put fingers to his teeth, and blew a quivering parody of a whistle.

The mouse-colored dot did not move.

Ramsey mustered saliva, soaked his lips, rolled his tongue around his mouth, and this time it was better, a loud, piercing sound.

He thought the gray dot moved. He whistled again. Then the dot was in full motion, trotting toward him through the hock-high grass. And as it neared, he saw that it was Gibson Girl, a nine-year-old mare. As she approached, she nickered curiously.

Meanwhile, Ramsey was busy. Grunting with effort, he unlatched the rope on his saddle, tied one end hard to the horn. Now, as the mare came up to the fence, he awkwardly tried to spread out a loop.

Gibson Girl backed away from the tangled wire and would not cross it. That was just as well, Ramsey thought; she'd only tangle herself hopelessly. But what he needed was for her to come to him through the gate.

So now he began to talk her to him, in a crooning, encouraging voice. She was gentle, well-trained and intelligent; there was no reason for her not to come; and in a moment, she trotted down the fence line, and Ramsey twisted to see what she would do.

She reached the gate; then she balked, planting her feet, tossing her head, snorting loudly. She did not like the dead man directly in her path; it was something new, frightening. Ramsey crooned to her desperately, but instead of moving forward, she snorted again and backed away.

She was spooky now, Ramsey saw despairingly. Though his throat was dry, he kept up his litany of encouragement and blandishment. Gibson Girl walled her eyes, trotted off in the direction from which she'd come, paused, snorted, and then came back toward the fence. But she halted well clear of it, liking that tangled wire and the carcass on the other side of it no better than she had the dead man. She was a good twenty feet away and nervous as a cat from the smell of death and the excitement of the night, and Ramsey knew she would come no closer and that it was now or never.

It would be the most important throw with a rope he had ever made—and the most impossible. Propped on one elbow, tangled in fence— But he whirled the loop a couple of times as best he could and prayed as he let it sail.

Maybe, he thought later, he was entitled to that much miracle after everything else. The loop sailed wide, but Gibson Girl was startled by it, jumped sideways, and rammed her head straight through it. As the line slid tight through the

24

honda, the mare, unused to being roped, gave way to panic and turned and tried to run. When she did, the rope snapped taut with strain, and as it brought her up short, her own weight lifted the dead horse by the saddle horn. Not much, but a fraction of an inch, and that was enough for Sam Ramsey to slide frantically out from under, tangled stirrup and all.

Then, gasping and exhausted, he fell back, while Gibson Girl fought nervously at the end of the line. He knew that he was in for pain, but how much, he could not guess. Until the blood started to flow, until the pain came, he did not even know whether he had a broken bone.

The pain came, all right, enough of it to make him grit his teeth and curse and hammer the ground with his clenched fists. Gibson Girl quit her fighting and stood motionless at rope's end, looking at him with ears pricked curiously.

After an eternity, the agony subsided a bit. Carefully, Ramsey untangled himself from the wire. Then, with tremendous effort, he got his good leg under him and pushed himself erect. But his knee buckled; he fell forward against a standing fence post and clung there.

At last, he tried his weight on his left leg. To his surprise, it bore him with no additional agony, and he let out a sound of relief—nothing was broken in it. He took a stumbling step, then another, and then another still; and at last he was leaning against Gibson Girl's withers, and she was nuzzling him gently.

When he could move freely again, he dragged the saddle off the dead gelding and put it on the mare. He found his empty Colt in the grass a dozen feet away, and reloaded it and thrust it in its holster. Then he examined the dead man.

In this sun, the body had already blackened and begun to swell, but the sightless eyes were blue, the hair and mustache fair, the clothes not Mexican, but ordinary Texas range garb. In the pockets there was nothing but a couple of gold double eagles, a few pesos, a hawk-billed knife, and cigarette makings.

The vultures were circling lower. Ramsey tied Gibson Girl up short and fought until he got the body up behind the saddle and lashed in place. Then he mounted and began the dismal circuit of his pastures.

They were empty, except for a handful of wild-eyed steers and the body of Dancing Man. A vulture dropping low led Ramsey to the carcass, its legs jutting stiffly. He dismounted and examined it, his mouth a thin line. The horse had been shot four times. Ramsey swore softly: Not only had the stal-

25

lion been immensely valuable, but he had raised and trained it from a foal. Fierce and aggressive in the protection of his mares from predators, Dancing Man had been as gentle with Ramsey as a pet dog. Ramsey looked up at the vultures and cursed them; but that was all he could do. Then he mounted up and rode on.

Geldings, mares, foals—they were all gone. The wire along the south side of the pasture had been cut for nearly two hundred feet, and the herd's trail was clear. Beyond the wire, chaparral began, a spiky wilderness of cactus and mesquite. This was part of Harrigan's ranch, overgrazed and gone to wasteland, a deserted corner never patrolled by Lazy H riders. Ramsey sketched a map of the country in his brain. Men who knew it could follow these thickets all the way across the Harrigan ranch and out the other side and still travel by daylight without too much fear of being spotted. Everything in Ramsey shrieked for him to plunge into the brush, along that clearly marked trail, but he kept Gibson Girl tight-reined. The rustlers had at least a six-hour start on him and they were ten or twenty to one against him. Then he pulled Gibson Girl around and made her give all she had on the ride to North Wells.

Sheriff Shan Williams said, "So they finally got around to you after all, huh?"

"That's right," Sam Ramsey said impatiently.

"Well, you got one of 'em anyway. That's better than Denning did."

"Goddammit, Shan," Ramsey said, "there ain't no time to stand here talkin'. If you can git some men together—"

Williams looked at him for a moment, dark eyes in a hawk's face expressionless. "From where?"

"From the town—"

"All right," Williams said. "I got two deputies here, and you and me, that makes four. And there's ten, twenty of 'em, you say?"

"Call Harrigan on the phone! Damn it, they crossed his land. Call Denning—this is his chance!"

"Yeah," Williams said. It was cool here in his thick-walled adobe office. He strode across it to a map of the county pinned on the wall. It covered a huge expanse; there were states in the Union smaller than this. "Six hours, you say, before you got loose from that dead horse. Another hour to git to town. Now, say, two hours at least to get some men together. That's nine hours start." He dragged his finger down the map. "Time for 'em to git down here, off the Lazy H, into this broken country. Even if we could swing around and cut 'em off there, which we'd have to kill the horses ridin' 'em to do, they could stand off an army in there. And do what they did to Tom and his bunch, just sift on out ahead of us, down into deep Big Bend, then across the Rio and into Mexico." He walked back to his desk and sat down. "It ain't no use, Sam."

"You're a hell of a sheriff, to talk that way!" Ramsey flared.

"I'll excuse that, Sam," Williams said calmly. "You're at the end of your string. But the fact remains, maybe I could git four, five men together. That ain't enough. Dammit, Sam, you wouldn't ride with Denning and them when they asked you. You think they're gonna saddle up again today and come running because *you've* been hit now? After just comin' back yesterday, dead-beat and two men lost?" He shook his head. "When I told 'em it was your stock we was after, they'd just laugh in my face."

Ramsey stared at him a moment. "I see," he said thinly.

"Sam, I know how you feel, but I can't do the impossible. If it was anybody but *you*—"

"I know," Ramsey said. "I know."

"Once the Rangers either catch or give up on Chico Cana, they've promised they'll come down in here and clean up this bunch. But Cana's killed men; these rustlers haven't. The Rangers gotta git him first, and they got every man they can muster pulled off station and patrollin' around Presidio, over west. Meanwhile, Tom and I wired the Governor, both Senators, and the Commandant at Bliss yesterday afternoon. Maybe in a week or two, the Army will—"

"In a week or two, my horses will be across the Rio." Ramsy stood there a moment, then sat down across the desk from Williams and lifted a penstaff out of its holder. "Shan, I'd like to borrow a piece of paper."

Williams blinked at him, then took a ruled tablet from his desk and passed it across.

Sam Ramsey began to write. For a long time the scratch of the pen was the only sound in the sheriff's office. Then Ramsey shoved the pad back across the desk. "Witness that for me, will you?"

Williams picked up what Ramsey had written and began to read, with a deepening frown.

"It's a will," Ramsey said. "If you witness it, it ought to be legal. I got this aunt in Pennsylvania—I never seen her, but she's my only living relative. If I don't come back in six months, sell my place at auction and send the money to her —there's the address down at the bottom."

Williams slapped down the pad. "Don't be a goddam fool,

27

Ramsey. You can't go down in that Big Bend country alone. Tom Denning went down there with twenty men, and you saw what happened to him!"

"I can't help it," Ramsey said. "The trail's still fresh and I got to follow it. Shan, I got to try to git my horses back."

"But not alone. Those rustlers and Mescans'll eat you alive." His voice was sharp, edged with authority. "No. I won't allow it."

"I don't know of any way you can stop me," Ramsey said.

Williams grinned without humor. "You forgot that dead body you brought in. We'll hold an inquest on it. But not for a week. Meanwhile, maybe I'll lock you up as a material witness. By then, maybe we'll have word from the Army—"

"Screw the Army," Ramsey said. "And don't you try to lock me up, Shan." His eyes were expressionless as he stood up.

Williams stared at him for a moment. Then he said, "All right, goddammit, it's your funeral. Go ahead."

"Thanks," Ramsey said wryly. Then, in a different tone, he said, "Don't forget, Shan. One man don't stir the dust of twenty."

"Nor throw the lead," Williams said heavily, getting up. Then he put out a hand. "All right, Sam. Good luck."

Ramsey took it. "Thanks, Shan. I'll be back when I find my horses."

"Yeah," Williams said, and he was still standing there when Ramsey turned and went out.

★   ★   ★

Impatient as he was, another full day passed before Ramsey could get under way. A man didn't go into bad country like that without careful preparation. Sam Ramsey's mind was methodical and dogged; maybe the horse-thieves would get him, but foolish to let the desert do their work for them.

The County Land Office had a few poor maps of the deep Big Bend—sketchy affairs compiled by the Army in the old Apache-chasing days. Ramsey studied them carefully.

The Big Bend country as a whole was an immense triangle within the sharp turn of the Rio Grande that gave the southern part of west Texas its outline. North Wells and the good ranching country around it filled part of the triangle's northeast corner. But, traveling south, the range land dwindled away; finally, about where the Santiago Mountains sliced across the region from northwest to southeast, it ended nearly completely, and the badlands began. It was the area south of the Santiagos that Ramsey studied intently on the maps. At least the main mountain ranges were indicated and the location of a few creeks, springs, and water holes—most of them, now, in early May, would be dry.

Still, rough as they were, the maps gave an indication of the immensity of that wasteland in the deep Big Bend. Three thousand or more square miles of mountains, deserts, and rock, with only a pathetic skein of rough trails leading to the few isolated ranches or the occasional mine within its reaches. Down there, he'd heard, there were arroyos that could swallow up the whole town of North Wells, canyons that could hide half the population of Texas. Across the border, there were armies of Mexican revolutionaries and gangs of bandits, even still a few bunches of half-wild Indians. There were wild horses and burros, deer and javelinas, mountain lions, rattlers, scorpions, and maybe even an occasional jaguar. And somewhere in there, as well, were the men who had his Morgans—men who were the last wild remnant of the old lawless days, outlaws and army deserters who preferred the bleak freedom of the desert to jail or hanging . . .

He had no idea how he was going to find them or what he would do when he did. All he knew was that he had to try to get his horses back.

Down in Mex town on the south side of North Wells, he bought four goatskin waterbags, checking them carefully for leaks or flaws. He had plenty of ammunition for the .45 and the Winchester at home, as well as the rest of the gear he needed.

Besides Gibson Girl, three geldings remained in his corral. One of these, Sunrise, was fully broken; the other two needed a lot of work, but they could be ridden and would do for pack animals. He worked far into the night assembling his outfit: pack saddles; bags of grain for the horses; guns and ammunition; binoculars; canteens; first-aid equipment; a light tarp for shelter against brutal sun or driving night wind; ropes, hobbles, picket pins . . . When he was finished, he showered—probably the last bath he'd have in weeks—and slept for three hours. He awakened with the sun, and it took him another hour to get the animals loaded. Then he mounted Gibson Girl and, leading his pack string, set out. There was an advantage to riding the mare—anxious to rejoin her bunch, she would serve almost as a bloodhound, helping to keep him to the trail, even if it dimmed.

He rode directly back to the pastures, where the vultures and coyotes had not left much of Dancing Man. Then he pushed through the gap in his fence and into Harrigan's chaparral.

The trail was a little wind-blown, yet still easy to read. But it was slow-going to follow it. The chaparral was a jungle of vicious thorns and barbs, and he did not want his horses torn by it. His jaw set as he saw that the raiders had not been troubled by such considerations; frequently, there were blood spots on the trail. The bastards, he thought. Every horse in that bunch will have fly-blown wounds in another day . . .

* CHAPTER FOUR *

He made poor time the first day. Unused to loads, the pack horses gave him continual trouble; moreover, the trail led through miles more of the nearly impenetrable tangle of mesquite and cactus. The second day was better; he came clear of the chaparral, and the land stretched open and rolling before him, with blue mountains in the distance. Those were the Santiagos, and once he was over them, he'd be truly in the badlands. It would be like crossing the Pecos in the old days, he thought; there was no law south of the Santiagos.

Now, hour by hour, the country changed. Grass and fences were far behind. This was a tableland of sand, gravel, creosote bush and prickly pear. Pointed toward the Santiagos, the trail, though wind-blown, was easy to read. The rustlers were sacrificing concealment to speed; and twice in those two days, Ramsey came across dead foals, already gnawed by vultures and coyotes. Too young to keep up with the herd, they'd been left where they'd fallen, and no one had even spent a cartridge to put them out of their misery. After each such discovery, Sam Ramsey would push his own animals hard, until common sense returned and he reined in to a saner gait.

On the second night, he camped within fifteen miles of the Santiagos, on the rim of a barranca forty feet deep, from the bottom of which welled a little spring. The herd had been watered here, and Ramsey found two more dead foals up the ravine. Though everything within him shrieked for him to move on, he made camp. The rustlers might have strung out sentries along their backtrail, and he did not want to overreach and run into them in darkness. Besides, he was getting an idea of the terrain ahead—a crazy-quilt of jumbled hills and draws and sand-flats . . . not the kind of country to take a half-raw pack-string through at night unless you wanted a broken neck at the bottom of some rockslide or had time to travel stupidly miles out of your way to a dead end in some box-canyon.

Besides, he was counting on the fact that the herd could not be pushed all the way to the Rio without halting for water and graze on the way. Somewhere south of the Santiagos, the rustlers would have to lay over for rest, or, in this country, they'd kill the horses. That would give him a chance to close the gap.

As the setting sun painted mountains and desert with fantastic colors, he oriented his map. The Chisos Mountains were the biggest range down there, and in their heart was a basin that had once been the hiding place of Apaches. Maybe there was graze and water there—if he lost the trail, that was where he would head.

The map—and what information he'd picked up here and there—told him little else. The old Comanche war trail, from Mexico to the Panhandle, was the one main road of this country, and keeping on in his present direction, he'd strike it tomorrow. From it fanned out a few pathetic trails after it had crossed the natural fortress of the Santiagos—they led, probably, to the five or six widely scattered ranches where a few hardy souls struggled to wrest enough graze from the desert to support a handful of cows and sheep. Far to the west, at Terlingua, there was a mine still in operation and a tiny settlement around it, another, also far west, at Study Butte. Less than a hundred inhabitants, all told, in those thousands of square miles, and below the Rio, it was even more desolate, the lone settlements of Boquillas and San Vicente hugging the river, and beyond them only uncounted miles of desert, mountains, and chaparral.

He made no fire. A can of cold beans and some leathery tortillas were his supper. After he had eaten, he drank freely from his canteen, knowing he could refill it at the spring. Then, with the hobbled horses making comfortable sounds in the darkness, he leaned back against his saddle and lit a cigarette.

Probably, he thought, he was as much fool as Shan Williams had called him. But he had to keep on, even if it meant he died out here, for without his horses, he had nothing and was nobody. If he did not get his horses back, he felt as if he would cease to exist anyway.

He had brought plenty of tobacco, and he lit another cigarette as soon as the first one was gone. It was not right, he thought, for a man's life to come only to that—a herd of horses and no more. But that was the way it was with him, and it was too late to help it. Maybe if things had been different fifty years ago, maybe if the Army had never sent his

31

father south; if it had only sent him to Wyoming or Montana instead—

By the time he finished the second cigarette, it had grown bitterly cold, and he put on his heavy jacket. The rising wind clashed and rattled the willows and cottonwood sprouts around the spring. Ramsey spread his blankets, hoping no side-winder or scorpion would come to share their warmth, lay down, pillowed his head against his saddle, and tried to sleep.

But, even trail-weary as he was, sleep was a long time coming. The wind played mournfully around outcroppings and updraws; it rustled creosote and rattled dried canes of ocotillo and the blades of yucca and Spanish bayonet. Animals were coming to drink at the spring, too; he heard a faint grunting and an occasional squeal down in the draw that meant javelinas, the lean, musky little wild pigs of the desert; once there was a snort that sounded like a startled deer. He had been through so much, had been so tense and alert all day that, as soon as he fell into a doze, the slightest sound brought him up with his hand on the holstered pistol near his head.

Presently, though, not even his taut-strung nerves could keep him awake any longer; at last he fell into a sleep as deep as if he'd been slammed over the head with a stone.

And when he awakened, it was daylight. He opened his eyes, and the first thing he saw was a pair of enormous, dusty black boots planted in the sand ten feet away; and the second thing was his own pistol, trained squarely at his head, the big gun almost lost in the huge, black hand that held it.

"Don't move," a deep voice said. "Jest lay there, mister."

At first Sam Ramsey, doped with sleep, had thought it was a dream. The voice drove all sleep from him and proved it wasn't. He opened his eyes wider, without lifting his head, and stared at the apparition between himself and the rising sun.

The Negro wore a straw sombrero, brim and crown alike tattered and frayed. His face was black as anthracite and glistening with sweat; his eyes were in shadow, but his thick lips were curled back in a kind of snarl and his teeth gleamed startlingly white. He was a giant of a man, with tremendous shoulders and lean, rawboned arms and legs; he wore a filthy flannel shirt, an equally filthy neckerchief draped around his neck, and a pair of tattered chaps. He was squatting flat-footed, like a Mexican, and the .45 in his hand did not waver.

Ramsey's heart sank. Well, it was over before it had begun. They had left someone to cover their backtrail farther back

32

than he had figured. And their lookout had taken him like a child snatching up a piece of candy.

"Awright," the Negro said. "Now that you awake, you can sit up. But no sudden moves."

Slowly, Ramsey raised himself. The dawn wind was chilly, and as the blanket fell away, he shivered.

The Negro tipped back the straw sombrero. Now Ramsey could see his eyes. There was killing in them.

"It feel different now, don't it, you white trash?" the Negro said. "The shoe on the other foot now, ain't it? How *you* like lookin' at your executioner?"

Ramsey blinked, not understanding.

Then the Negro called, not loudly, but in a voice that carried, "Awright, Noracita. Everything under control now."

Ramsey could not control a start of surprise when a woman's voice answered from down in the barranca. "Coming, Concho."

At Ramsey's confusion, something glinted in Concho's eyes. "Y'all give up too soon, didn't you? You almost had us one time, but we holed up and you rode right by. But it didn't matter, anyhow—you knew we couldn't live out on the desert with no water and no horses and only five bullets in the gun. You thought the desert would take good care of us and you wouldn't never hafta worry about witnesses. But you was wrong, white man—and before I git through with you, you're gonna know just how wrong you really was!"

"I got no idea what you're talkin' about," Ramsey heard himself say. Then motion in the gently sloping draw that led down to the spring caught his eyes. Despite the gun, he sat up quickly and very straight as the woman came into view.

The sun had burnt her so dark, it was hard to tell whether she was white, Indian, or Mexican. She wore a straw sombrero like the Negro's, a denim brush-jacket, a long, divided leather skirt, and riding boots. She stopped for a moment, staring at the two men, and then she came toward them wearily, as if she were sore-footed. She took a position beside the Negro, whose height dwarfed her, and now Ramsey saw that she had chestnut hair and gray eyes and that her features were completely Caucasian. In fact, she must once have been very pretty; but now she was tired and drawn and powdered with dust. Her bosom was full beneath the brush-jacket and the smeared white shirt under it; her waist slender, and there was a good curve to her hips. He could not really tell, but if she were over thirty, Ramsey would have been wrong in his guess. He had no more idea what she was doing here than if some kind of flying machine had suddenly descended onto the desert.

"Look at 'im," Concho said, without turning his head. "Ain't he one of 'em?"

The woman was silent for a moment. Then she said, in a soft, husky, very weary voice, "I don't know."

"He bound to be," Concho said.

"I don't know," the woman said again. "I thought I never would forget any of them, but I don't remember him."

"That cut no ice," Concho said. "Blood for blood, anyhow." Until now, the pistol had not been cocked. It clicked as the big thumb eared back the hammer.

"Wait," the woman said. Her voice trembled. "I don't want to see it. I've seen all I want to see; I can't watch this."

"Then you go over yonder or back down to the water. I'm gonna make him stand up, clear of them blankets and that saddle, cause we don't wanta ruin them. Then I gonna shoot him. I think that only fair, don't you?"

"Concho—" she said hesitantly.

"You go back down to the water and put yo' fingers in yo' ears. He gonna holler awhile."

The air was full of the smell of death. Ramsey was trembling. The woman did not move. "Git up!" Concho snapped. "Stand up slow and easy."

Ramsey pulled himself up out of the blankets. His legs were shaking and he had a terrible need to make water. He was afraid to speak lest it trigger the fatal shot, and yet, even in his fear, outrage was burning in him; and suddenly he heard his own voice, rasping, angry, and astonishingly controlled. "Goddammit, don't I even get a chance to talk?"

"How much chance y'all give Hank Stewart?" Concho said, rising to six and a half feet of height, a terrible blackness against the lightening sky.

"Who the hell's Hank Stewart? Another one of your horse-thief gang? He the one I shot the other night in my pasture?"

Suddenly the woman stepped around beside Concho to confront Ramsey. She barely came up to the Negro's biceps. She put a hand on Concho's left wrist. "Wait a minute," she said.

"No need to wait. This buzzard—"

"I said 'wait!'" This time she snapped it, and it was an order.

Concho hesitated. Then he said grudgingly, "Yes, ma'am." But he did not lower the gun.

The woman took a step closer to Ramsey, peering at him closely. Then she said, very softly, "I don't think you were at the ranch." Then she asked: "Who are you and what are you doing here?"

He licked dry lips, aware that the determination in Concho's eyes had not abated. "My name's Ramsey. I'm trailing a bunch of stolen horses—"

"Morgans?"

He forgot Concho, then. "You've seen 'em?"

She did not answer that. She stepped back. "His saddle stock and pack animals," she said to Concho, jerking her head. "Morgans like the ones Kelly was driving."

"Who's Kelly?" Ramsey blurted, but they ignored him.

"That cut no ice," Concho said. He still had the gun up. "All the same, he could have been at the ranch. 'Sides, we need his gear."

"Where're you from?" the girl asked.

"North Wells."

"You know a man there, a big man that brought a bunch of people in here—his name's Tom something."

"Denning."

"Why weren't you with his crowd?"

"I don't travel with any crowd."

The woman looked at Concho and shook her head. "He wasn't there," she said. "I'll swear to it."

"You can't know everybody was there. He may be lyin'."

"This ranch," Ramsey said, "that you keep talkin' about. What happened there?"

"Those riders from North Wells," the woman said tonelessly, "murdered my husband."

Ramsey only stared at her for a moment. Denning had—?

She went on, her voice still oddly flat. "My name's Nora Stewart. We had a little ranch southeast of the Chisos. Not much, but it kept us alive. Me, Hank—my husband." Here for the first time, her voice faltered. She swallowed hard. "And Concho," she added.

Her breasts rose as she sucked in a deep breath. "Ten days ago this man Denning and his outfit came back across the border. They'd had a fight, were all shot up. Like a bunch of . . . of hydrophobic wolves, ready to slash at anything. They . . . they accused us of being in with Sheep Kelly and his bunch and . . . they hanged my husband and burned the ranch. Tore down our windmill, killed all our saddle stock . . ." Her voice shook and faded, whether because of anger or grief, he could not tell. "No trial, no anything, wouldn't even listen to Hank. Just . . . strung him up to the shed rafters like . . ." She shook her head and broke off.

"Denning came back to North Wells," Ramsey said. "He never mentioned nothing like this."

"A man tell murder on hisself?" Concho sneered. "They

35

was gonna hang me, too, and maybe Miss Nora, for all I know. But I busted out from 'em and took Nora with me." There was savage triumph on his face. "Killed one a them bastards, too. Jest one good hit with my fist."

"Denning lost two men. Said to Mescans near San Vicente."

"He only lost one to them. Lost the other to me," Concho said proudly.

"No wonder Billy Goodhue was primed to explode," Ramsey said.

"What?" Concho wagged the gun.

"Nothing," Ramsey said. Then he said, "I've got a horse ranch near North Wells. Denning wanted me to go with 'em, but I turned him down. I wasn't at your ranch. I didn't know anything about that killing."

"Then what you doin' down here?"

"Three nights ago a gang hit my spread, lifted my whole herd of Morgans. If I don't git 'em back, I'm ruined. They didn't bother to hide the trail, and it's brought me this far."

"By yourself?" Concho's tone was incredulous.

"Nobody else to come with me. I—ain't very well liked in North Wells."

"You gonna be liked a whole lot less when we come ridin' in on your horses and give that Mister Denning what he got comin' to him," Concho said. "He owes us for one murder, a whole ranch layout, and better'n a hundred head of cows."

"He ran off your stock?"

"No. But now that Hank's dead, Sheep Kelly'll snatch 'em up and them Mescans'll fill enchiladas with 'em. He owes us for somethin' else, too—ten days out in the desert on foot with no canteens an' mighty little to eat."

Ramsey blinked. "For God's sake, how'd you live ten days in this hell like that?"

Concho grinned without humor. "Travelin' at night. I know ever' water hole and spring in the Big Ben country. If I didn't, we'da been dead two days after we got loose. And I took me a six-shooter off that guard I mashed. Wa'n't but five bullets, and we used all them up, but enough to get us a little meat now and then." He looked at Ramsey's heaped gear. "We gonna travel the resta the way to North Wells in style."

Ramsey said, "You will if you kill me. But that's the only way."

"I ain't particular," Concho said. "I got me a mad on and I'd jest as soon kill you as anybody I know, except for that Denning *hombre*."

"You'll have to do it," Ramsey said. "Because I came here after my horses and I ain't turning back. And I figure it'll take every bit of outfit I brought with me to do what I come to do."

The woman had sat down, resting her head in her hands as if unutterably weary. Now she spoke again.

"Look," she said, "just give us a little food and lend us one of your horses. You do that, and we'll make it to North Wells."

"Maybe," Ramsey said. "But you'll never make it out of North Wells again."

"You think not?" Concho's grin was like that of a wolf.

"You won't," Ramsey said. "Not if what you told me was true. There are eighteen men in North Wells that were mixed up in that hanging. They didn't report it when they came in —they was over their madness by then and must have realized what they did. Not only hangin' a man without a trial, but leavin' a woman to die in the desert. They won't want that gettin' out." His mind had grasped the facts now, and suddenly he was beginning to see how—if these two did not kill him—he might gain advantage from this meeting. "You" —he pointed at Concho—"you think the minute you show up in North Wells, they won't recognize you and kill you? You won't get to first base against Denning and that bunch." He paused. "Not without help."

Nora Stewart had been listening intently. Now she said, "Mister, you're driving at something. Help. What kind of help?"

For the first time in this encounter, Sam Ramsey was able to smile faintly. "If you'll make him put down my gun, we'll cook up some coffee and some breakfast and I'll tell you. Then, if you still want to kill me, at least I'll have had a last meal."

Her gray eyes locked with his for a long moment. Her burnt and dusty face was expressionless, unreadable. Then, almost imperceptibly, she nodded.

"Put the gun away, Concho," she said quietly, without looking at the Negro. "And let this gentleman make us some breakfast. I'm starving."

★ CHAPTER FIVE ★

Ramsey was hungry, too, and the three of them ate like wolves. When the last bit of bacon grease had been sopped

37

from the skillet and one final pot of coffee bubbled on the coals, Ramsey took out makings. Nora Stewart let out a sigh. "I'm almost beginning to feel human again."

Ramsey poured another cup of coffee and passed it to Nora. She drank it hungrily. For a while, the three of them sat in an odd, suspended silence. Then Nora had finished the coffee and passed the cup back to Ramsey and some light had come into her eyes. She even smiled a little, and she looked oddly shy. "One more thing," she said hesitantly. "You wouldn't happen to have soap . . . and a towel?"

Ramsey said, "Sure." Again he searched the bag, brought out a small, worn towel and a bar of Octagon and passed them to her. She got stiffly to her feet. "I'm going to have a bath," she said to Concho. "I've just got to have a bath."

"Go ahead," Concho said. She started for the draw that led down to the spring, and Concho pulled Ramsey's Colt from his waistband and laid it on his thigh, its muzzle pointing to Ramsey and his big hand covering grip and cylinder loosely. As Nora moved out of earshot, Concho said quietly: "Mister, if you even look towards that arroyo while she's down there, I'll blow you to kingdom come."

Ramsey said, "What do you think I am?" He poured the cup full of coffee and passed it to Concho. But he could not help thinking about her down there . . . He frowned at Concho.

"You say they hanged Stewart for being in with Sheep Kelly. Who's Sheep Kelly, and was Stewart really in with him?"

"Sheep Kelly's the man's gonna kill you if you keep on after him," Concho said. "And no, Stewart wasn't in with him. I mean, he didn't make no money out of Sheep. Of course he had to buy supplies for Sheep and his outfit and let 'em water at his ranch when they come through with thirsty stock, but there wasn't no way around that. Had to, or Sheep woulda wiped him out and took his woman. Only way to keep his goods and his wife was to do that—but you don't hang a man for doin' what he can't help."

"What about you? You worked for Stewart? Why didn't you throw in with Kelly instead of wanderin' around the desert?"

"Two reasons. Kelly from Alabama and he can't abide folks my color and I can't abide bastards like him. Other reason, Miss Nora. She hate Sheep Kelly's guts; with her man dead, she wouldn't go near Kelly. And where she go, I go. It been like that for a long, long time. Besides, we got a score to settle in North Wells."

Ramsey stared at him for a moment. Then he asked,

38

"What's a woman like her doing on a desert ranch anyhow? She doesn't look the kind would be happy out here in this hell-hole."

Concho's face, which had relaxed a little, now hardened to a black mask, and suddenly his eyes were cold and deadly. "I reckon there ain't one bit of that that's any of your business, Mister Man." And Ramsey saw that his hand had tightened on the Colt.

"All right, forget it," Ramsey said. He took the empty coffee cup, rinsed it with water from a canteen, and poured himself coffee. "Let's go back to Kelly. Who is he? What am I up against?"

"You up against a lotta bad men," Concho said, almost with satisfaction. "Kelly, he's a deserter from the cavalry. He killed a man in some kinda barracks-room brawl and checked out ahead of a court-martial and a firing squad. Come down here into Big Bend and holed up. There already more than a few deserters down in here, but they just little bitty operators until Kelly come in. Maybe they shoot some prospector and lift his grubstake or steal a beef or two or maybe even a mine payroll if they're feelin' biggity. But Kelly, that penny-ante stuff ain't for him. All this fightin' and revolution start in Old Mexico, them armies just pick all the northern states along the Rio Bravo clean as a whistle, and still they got to have somethin' to eat and somethin' to ride, and they got *mucho pesos* to pay for it. That when Kelly start liftin' stock outside and runnin' it through here to the border."

"How many men has he got?"

Concho grinned. "However many he needs. Maybe fifteen, twenty whites his own stripe. But these Mescan *buscaderos,* they'll lend him more any time he needs 'em."

"To fight on this side of the border?"

"Sho. Kelly's valuable to 'em, he's their supply line. And gringo beef tastes better anyhow. That Denning and his people, they just lucky they didn't bump into Kelly. Sheep coulda had a hundred Mexes detached for service under him, and it woulda been a short horse and soon curried if it had been him Denning's crowd hit up against. Instead, they just bumped into some big *Revolucionario* patrol across the river and got away after a measly little fight. But Kelly, he's an old-time cavalry first sergeant. If he'd been in command, he'da surrounded and wiped 'em out before you could say Jack Robinson."

He paused. "Now, mister, you understand why you might jest as well turn around without any fuss and all three of us ride back to North Wells? This ole Big Bend ain't no place at all for one lone man, no matter how big the ideas he's got."

39

He looked at Ramsey appraisingly. "You ain't any kind of gunhand, neither. If you was, I'd never have slipped that fawty-five away from you. I bet you never even been in a gunfight."

"I was in one a few nights ago."

"You kill yo' man yet?"

Sam said: "Then. One of Kelly's."

Concho smiled condescendingly. "Yo' first?"

"Yeah," Sam grunted.

"Kelly got plenty more where he come from."

"I can't help that," Ramsey said.

Concho began to make another cigarette. "You are a *dee*-termined man, ain't you?"

"I aim to git my horses back," Sam Ramsey said.

* * *

The woman came up the draw from the spring. As she stepped into full view, Sam Ramsey, despite himself, gaped.

She had washed her hair, and the long chestnut fall of it, still in damp strings, cascaded down her back and caught the glint of sunlight. Her tanned face shone with cleanliness, and there was a new sparkle to her eyes. She had washed out the white blouse and put it back on herself to dry and carried her hat in hand and her brush-jacket over her arm; and the damp fabric of the blouse molded itself to breasts that were large and rich and rounded. There were new life and vitality in her eyes and face and in her step as well; and now Sam Ramsey could see that, even under these circumstances, she was more than ordinarily pretty; she had beauty.

She sat down on Ramsey's blanket next to the fire, cross-legged, and gave her head a shake that fanned the hair into the full light and heat of the sun. Her eyes were large and their lashes long; her nose was straight, almost aristocratic, her lips perfectly shaped and red, her chin firm. Though she was bronzed, her skin had not yet taken on that leathery texture common to most ranch women. Ramsey revised his estimate of her age; she was not more than twenty-five.

She said, "I don't guess you've got a comb or brush."

"A brush." He reached in his sack and handed it to her, and her look of delight at the sight of it was completely feminine. She began to brush her hair, and Ramsey stared at her, feeling a completely involuntary thrust of desire. Then he became aware of Concho's gaze on him, hard, cold, threatening and jealous, and he wrenched his eyes away. The business of making a cigarette bridged a tense interval.

Then Ramsey said, not particularly to Concho, "We're

back to where we started from. You want to go to North Wells and I want to find my horses." He blew smoke. "I've got a proposition to make you two."

Concho's voice had fresh hostility in it. "Mister, you in no position to make anybody propositions."

"All the same, I'm gonna do it. Concho, I'll say it again. You can kill me and take my horses and goods, but you ride into North Wells or even near it, nobody but you and her, and you'll be a dead man and no telling what'll happen to her, long before you ever get to Tom Denning. Denning's the big dog in the whole country. He knew what he did here was murder, but neither him nor any of his men have ever breathed a word of it. Against him and the other big ranchers, you won't have the chance of a snowball in hell—by yourself."

"As good a chance as you got against Kelly by *yourself*."

"I won't argue that," Ramsey said. "That's my whole proposition. You help me, I'll help you."

"You go to—" Concho began, but Nora Steward had laid aside the brush and was staring at Ramsey. "Hush a minute, Concho," she said.

Then she asked Ramsey, "Just what do you mean?"

Cautiously, Ramsey stood up. "I'll never catch Kelly by followin' his trail; he'll always be ahead of me. But he's got to stop and water and graze those horses somewhere and—" He looked directly at Concho. "And I'll bet a purty you know where."

Concho did not answer that.

"I need a guide," Ramsey said. "Somebody to take me the short way to wherever Kelly will stop with my horses before he pushes on across the Rio. I'm not asking anybody to fight for me or to take any chances for me—all I want is somebody to swing me out ahead of Kelly to make up for the time I've lost. From then on, I'll be on my own."

"And dead in jig time," Concho said.

"That's a chance you'll have to take. If I am, you've lost nothing. You'll still have my horses and outfit. You can still go on to North Wells, only a few days late."

"And—suppose for the sake of supposin'—you do come out alive?" Concho asked. "What great benefit we gonna git then?"

Sam Ramsey said, "You get my protection when we all three ride into North Wells together."

"Your protection? And jest who the hell are you?" Concho's face twisted in a sneer.

Ramsey looked down at him, and now his voice crackled. "All right," he snapped, "I'm gonna give it to you straight.

41

You're a nigger, Concho, and anybody in North Wells that wants to shut your mouth can fill you full of lead and nobody's gonna worry any more about it than if you were a stray dog."

Concho sprang to his feet. "Why, you goddamned—"

"Shut up and let me finish!" Ramsey flared. "Niggers and Mexicans are fair game in a town like North Wells—and so's any white woman that runs around alone with a black man. The minute you're spotted by anybody that remembers you —and don't forget, there's eighteen of 'em—you're a dead man, no questions asked. And as for her"—he jerked his head toward Nora—"they ain't goin' to ask her but one question: *What were you and that nigger doin' out there in that desert together all that time?* And they'll answer it their way and she'll be rousted out of town before your corpse is cool!"

Concho stood there with his eyes savage and his black face working, glistening with sweat. His fingers were curling and opening and curling again around the Colt he held at his side.

"You don't stand a chance of gettin' at Denning by yourself," Ramsey went on harshly. "You need a white man's protection. The people in North Wells don't like me worth a damn, but they know my word's good and they respect me. If we go to Sheriff Shan Williams and I speak for you and lay your charges in front of him, then it's a law matter."

"A law matter," Concho snapped. "That's dandy, ain't it?"

"Williams deputized those men. They were actin' under his authority. But he didn't authorize a lynchin', and when he finds out they committed one while wearin' his badges and lied to him in the bargain about it, he's man enough to see they're brought to trial. All of 'em. Maybe it'll never go past that, maybe they'll all be acquitted, but at least the truth will be out and they'll have to live with it. And maybe that'll be more hell in the long run than they bargained for."

Concho spat. "Trial," he said, and spun the cylinder of the Colt.

"You going to kill all eighteen of 'em?" Ramsey asked with biting sarcasm. "You know what they'll do to you after being alone with a white woman?"

For a moment, the campsite there on the rim of the barranca was silent, the three figures poised in the glaring sun. Then Concho raised the gun. "Mister," he said, and now the intent on his face was beyond question, "you done signed your own death warrant with that foul mouth of your'n. Nobody talks about this lady that way and lives." He eared back the hammer to full cock. And in that instant, Nora Stewart sprang between him and Ramsey, so that the gun was pointed at her breast.

"Put that thing down, Concho," she snapped, "and don't be a fool!"

He reached out with one big hand. "Miss Nora, you stand clear."

"No! Don't you see that he's right?"

"Ain't nobody goin' to even *hint* about you—"

"Stop it and put up that gun!" she commanded. "You think that after where we came from that talk bothers me? Ramsey's right; we need him. Put it away, Concho!"

The huge Negro stood there tensely, not moving, only his face working curiously. Then his giant frame trembled strangely and the hand holding the gun dropped. "Noracita," he said, and his voice had gone gentle. "Noracita, I was only trying to protect—"

"I know," she said. She put out a hand and took the Colt from him and he offered no resistance. Deftly, she eased the hammer down and handed the gun butt-first to Ramsey. "Here," she said. Her eyes met his directly. "This puts us at your mercy. Concho used all the cartridges we had to feed us."

His eyes still locked with hers, marveling at the beauty of her and at the iron in her beneath the surface, Sam absently stuck the Colt in his belt. "There's plenty more in that bag yonder," he heard himself say, "if that's a .45 he's carrying. He can help himself."

"It's not important," she said. And she turned away. "He can load up after we talk," she said.

It was she and Ramsey who did the talking. Concho sat apart, long arms locked around bony knees, face shadowed and unreadable under his hat brim, though Ramsey could feel the pressure of glowering, inimical eyes.

She had married Hank Stewart two years before, Nora said. "He was . . . a good man." Her voice did not quite falter. "As good as any woman could want. He was a *kind* man; there aren't many of those. And the people who killed him are going to pay for it, one way or another. He was ready to feed them and shelter them and . . . and they hanged him and burned everything he had built and ran off his stock and . . . You couldn't *live* in this country without making some kind of peace with Sheep Kelly, but that didn't mean he was a rustler." She shook her head. "Anyway, we're going to hold you to it. You're our passport out of this desert and you're to speak for us in North Wells when we make our charges."

"I gave you my word," Ramsey said. "But first, my horses."

"We saw Kelly pass with them," Nora said.

"What kind of shape were they in?"

"He'd been pushing them hard. They looked like what Hank would have called ganted. That's all I can tell. We were holed up in some rocks on a butte; they went by on the flat below us."

"Headed where? The Chisos basin?" And Ramsey looked at Concho.

The Negro did not speak. After a moment, Nora said, gently: "Concho."

"Naw," Concho said grudgingly. "Not the basin. That's too much of a trap. He'll swing around between the Chisos and Chilicotal Mountain and into Juniper Canyon, where he can git 'em out in a hurry. There ain't much graze there, but there's water at this time of year in some creeks that come down outa the Chisos. And there's peaks he can put lookouts on where they can see clear to the Santiagos and spot anybody comin'. Then he'll send somebody on ahead across the Rio to contact the Mescans and probably turn the herd over at San Vicente. Then he and his outfit'll probably hole up in the usual place at the old mine on the toe of Mariscal, where there's some old 'dobe shacks and it's not a long jump across the border. All them places are like forts," he said, his voice cutting. "Whole goddam United States Cavalry couldn't take them horses from him in there. I don't see how *you* figger to do it."

"Neither do I," Ramsey said evenly. "But that's my worry, not yours. All I'm askin' you to do is guide me so I can look over the situation and figure out what to do. Can you swing me around so I can get there while the horses are still there without being spotted?"

Concho spat. "They'll be close to there now. We'll hafta ride like bastards. But I kin do it. We'll cut through the Santiagos at Dog Canyon an' go down Tornillo Creek. If we don't run into any Mescans comin' up from Boquillas, we can wait 'til we're past Chilicotal and swing west, but that'll hafta be at night. Daytime, we'd be spotted sure. Any water we git between now and then, we'll hafta dig outa the creek bed, and we won't dare a fire." He spat again. "There used to be a customs station at the Boquillas Ford, but it's been shut down for years. The Mescans killed the last coupla agents th' government sent in. The Mexes cross there and at San Vicente and range anywhere they want to, now."

"Who buys from Kelly? Villa?"

"Sometimes," Concho said. "Sometimes it's another bully boy, kinda tin-horn Villa named Leon Sanchez. Each one of 'em commands his own outfit, but they work together.

44

Mostly, Villa works farther west and it's Sanchez raises hell around here."

He stood up, went to a canteen, and drank long and deeply. Lowering it, he said, "That's another goddam thing —excuse me, Miss Nora. That man Denning can't kill us no deader than Kelly, or especially if we bump into some Mescans. Even in the best of times, they wouldn't balk at knockin' off a couple of *Norte Americanos* for horses, guns and . . . and for a woman like Miss Nora. But right now, they just like a swarm of stirred-up bees, anyhow. This business of Americans takin' over Vera Cruz has 'em ready to shoot any gringos on sight, no holds barred and no questions asked." He rinsed his mouth and spat a stream into the sand. "It's jest too damned dangerous to go back in yonder, and we ain't gonna do it, Miss Nora. I never steered you wrong yet, and I ain't steerin' you wrong now. Don't listen to what this *hombre* tells you. We'll take a coupla his horses and enough outfit to git us to North Wells, and don't you worry about the situation there, I'll handle it. You know I kin do it—and without any help from him, either."

Nora Stewart was silent for a moment, and then she shook her head. "No," she said; and there was a ring of iron in her voice.

Concho turned, setting down the canteen. "What you mean, no?"

"He's right. Do you think I'm going to let them get away with what they did to Hank? Do you think I'm not going to make them pay? Oh, they'll pay, all right—but we need him to help us see that they do." Her hands were clenching and unclenching. "You know how it's been, Concho. You know these Texas towns. Why do you think Hank chose the desert? We need somebody . . . somebody they'll listen to in North Wells. And we can't expect Ramsey to help us unless we help him."

"Dammit, Noracita—"

She flung her head around, eyes alight. "Concho, you heard me. I've made up my mind."

The huge Negro stood there, staring from Nora to Ramsey. His eyes, focused on Ramsey, were lambent with rage and hatred. But he drew in a breath that made his great chest swell, and then he let it out with a shuddering sound, and he said: "All right, Miss Nora."

Nora Stewart looked away from him. "Besides," she said in a thin voice, "we owe Sheep Kelly something, too. It was Denning that hanged Hank. But it was Sheep that drew down the lightning. If it hadn't been for Sheep, we could have lived

45

forever in peace." She looked at Ramsey. "We're ready to go," she said tonelessly, "when you are."

Ramsey got to his feet. He went to a pannier, fished inside it, took out a box of cartridges, and tossed them to Concho, who caught them deftly. "Load up," he said. "I'll be packing the animals."

Concho took his own pistol from his waistband and began pushing cartridges through the loading gate. "We're all a bunch of goddam fools," he grumbled, "and none of us'll come outa this goddam desert alive." He snapped the loading gate shut and spun the cylinder, then thrust the Colt back into his waistband. His eyes met those of Ramsey and challenged him. "Mister Man," he said harshly, "you better remember one thing. If anything happens to Miss Nora on accounta you, you'll pay for it. You hear?"

"I hear," said Ramsey coolly, and he turned away, whistling up the horses.

★ CHAPTER SIX ★

The Santiagos, as Ramsey's map showed and Concho verified, were pierced by two small gaps. The most northerly one, Persimmon Gap, was the main route into the Big Bend country; through it, the old Comanche war trail from the Panhandle to Mexico had passed, and now there was a travesty of a wagon road. Ramsey and Concho agreed that they dare not use it, though the rustlers had almost arrogantly swung the horses around that way. Instead, Concho led them farther to the southeast, across shimmering flats of creosote and cactus, to where a dry stream-bed pierced the barrier ridges through a gap called Dog Canyon. There might be lookouts here, too, but they had to cross the Santiagos somewhere, and it was a chance they had to take.

The mountains were, of course, farther away than they had looked; out here, everything was. By noon, they still had not reached Dog Canyon, and the mid-May heat had become almost unbearable. The horses were drenched with sweat, and so were their riders. Concho rode ahead; then came Nora Stewart, and Ramsey brought up the rear, leading the one heavily burdened pack horse. He was beginning to be concerned about Nora Stewart. He had given her Gibson Girl and the only saddle; he and Concho rode with makeshift pads. But it was obvious that the days she had already spent

46

in the desert had brought the woman almost to the end of her strength, and this journey in the worst part of the heat was sapping the rest of it. She rode with head down and shoulders slumped, and there were times when she swayed so violently in the saddle that it seemed she would fall. Then he would push his mount quickly up alongside hers; and she would straighten up and give him an enigmatic, defiant look, as if she refused to betray weakness or cry for consideration because of her sex.

Sometimes Concho would twist in the saddle and catch Ramsey riding alongside her. Then the Negro's hooded eyes would flare again with that lambent hatred; Ramsey had it diagnosed now, and knew it was jealousy, and when he would let his mount drop back, he would look from Nora to Concho thoughtfully.

At last, they reached the mouth of the canyon. The stream-bed ran fairly close to its right wall, which was really the toe of a harsh and barren mountain, and the shade of the towering rock was blessed. They had not gone far into the gap when Concho reined in and swung down. Ground-hitching the horse, he strode back to give Nora a hand down from the saddle. Then he turned to Ramsey.

"We got to hold up," he said defiantly, as if waiting for Ramsey to contradict him. "Me and this lady walked all last night; she ain't had no sleep since yesterday. Besides, these ain't desert horses; they got a lotta lard to bake out, still. We'll stay here 'til sunset."

"I can go on," Nora Stewart protested. "I can—"

"'Til sunset," Concho repeated with determination. "We got maybe forty miles more to go, roundabout, 'til we git within range of where they'll stop with the herd. And we might bump into somebody we gotta run from most anytime. Might as well pace ourselves so these hawses are fresh." He unrolled the blankets from behind her saddle and spread them on the sand. "You lay down here," he said to Nora in a gentle voice; and he helped her out of the brush-jacket and folded it into a pillow for her.

Nora protested no more. She stretched out on the blankets and closed her eyes. Her hair fanned out over the blanket, and her breasts rose and fell beneath the clinging, sweat-dampened shirt. Ramsey's gaze was drawn to her, then he was aware of Concho's presence. He turned, to face savagery in a stare. But all Concho said was, "We better give these hawses a little drink."

Using his Stetson for a pail, Ramsey gave each of the animals about a pint. As Concho replugged the goatskin, the Negro said: "We got to watch our water. This is the tail end

47

of the dry season, and there's damn little down here that ain't dried up."

Ramsey squinted at the slice of brassy sky he could see above the canyon walls. There was no promise of rain anywhere in it; and that, he reflected, was probably just as well. At least the danger of flash floods was eliminated. When rain came down here, nothing trapped it or held it back. Pouring off every barren slope and down every naked sheet of rock, by the time it hit the dry stream-beds, more often than not it had mounted into a thundering wall of water. Here in a place like this canyon, a rain thirty miles away could send a flood roaring at them without warning. And that, he thought, was typical of this damned country. Either too much or not enough—and either way, you could die from it.

Concho threw himself down on the sand in a shady place. "I gotta have a little bit of sleep, too. But we're where we oughta keep a lookout now. You slept last night—why don't you go down to the south end of the canyon, keep your eyes open? I'll be down in a coupla hours and relieve you."

Ramsey hesitated, resentment at taking orders from Concho rising. Then he shrugged; the Negro was right. He picked up a canteen and his field glasses and mounted Gibson Girl. Behind him, Concho was already stretched out and snoring.

It was a quarter of a mile to the mouth of the canyon. There, Ramsey ground-reined the horse in the shade and moved out beyond the canyon walls into the protection of a cluster of boulders, some of them higher than his head. Climbing up on one, he stretched out flat and scanned the vast expanse of territory before him with the glasses.

It was an awesome sight. Sun glittered off the cactus-choked flats. Humps of sand, gravel, and talus, their flanks bare of all but the harshest vegetation, mountains, mesas, draws and arroyos—as far as the eye could see all jumbled together in a stark, forbidding, sun-blasted, senseless mixture. And dominating it all, on the southern horizon, the shimmering, purplish saw-toothed bulk of the Chisos range. It was, Ramsey thought, hell's own country if there ever was one, a place designed by the devil for his private use. But sometimes he leased it out to favorites—Comanches, Apaches, and now Mexican bandits and horse-thieves.

Looking at that great, hostile jungle of eroded and merciless terrain, Ramsey understood all at once why Concho had thought him a fool. For one man to brag that he would go alone into such a place and wrest, single-handed, half a hundred horses from the grip of a dozen or more desperate men —that was purest loud-mouthed idiocy. More than that. It was suicide. Ramsey saw that now, and his courage faltered.

48

And yet, he thought, as he swept it all with the glasses and saw nothing more suspicious than a circling hawk, he had no alternative. Partly it was the kind of man he was; he tried to wrong no one and he would not tolerate being wronged himself. But even more than that, it was lack of any other anchor to life. Without wife, children, friends, he had invested himself totally in those Morgans. They were a part of him—a part that it was utterly necessary for him to get back. But how he would do it—? He had no idea, and it took an effort to fight back a wave of despair. I'll worry about that when the time comes, he told himself; but it was not a satisfactory answer.

Satisfied that the way in front of them was clear, he slid off the rock and found, gratefully, a pool of shade. There he sprawled and tried not to think. But that was impossible, too; somehow, a vision of Nora Stewart kept coming into his mind. Who was she, anyhow, and how had a woman like her wound up on a shirttail ranch deep in the heart of the badlands? And Concho, that huge, hostile, protective, rawboned black giant. What was his relationship to her? Concho was playing more than the role of loyal servant. *Let it ride,* he told himself fiercely; *let it ride.*

To break the train of thought, he climbed back up on the rock, scanned the terrain again, found nothing, and slid down. That set the pattern for the next two hours, while Gibson Girl, hot, hungry, and thirsty, jingled her bit chains impatiently.

Then she raised her head, ears pricked, and looked back down the canyon. There was the scrape of shod hoof on rock, and as Ramsey jumped to his feet, hand on his Colt, Concho rode around a turn in the canyon on a gelding. He came up, swung down, and gave Ramsey an inquiring look. "All clear?"

"Nothin' movin' that I can see."

Concho grunted. "Sheep Kelly's men like Apaches used to be. It when you *can't* see nothin' they most likely to be around. Well, you want some rest, go git it. I'll take over." He allowed himself a sardonic grin. "Okay, Mister Man, you done seen what's out there, what kinda hell's half-acre we got to ride through to find them damned horses of yourn. What you think of it?"

"Rough country," Ramsey said.

"You damn right. And I'm gonna tell you again, you ain't got a Chinaman's chance in it. Maybe if you was a professional, you could do it. But you ain't nothin' but a rancher."

Ramsey's eyes narrowed. "A professional what?"

"Fightin' man," Concho said.

49

"You think you're one?"

Concho's grin widened, though still ugly. "Listen, mister, I started out sixteen years ago, Tenth Cavalry in Cuba. Then I fought in the ring for better'n two years, New York, Chicago. But got tired of cities, drifted on down to Mexico, hired out in a private army a silver mine kept. But had some trouble, killed a man, then I took off, met up with Pancho Villa. Rode with his bunch a while, but got fed up with Mexico. Come back to the States, Baton Rouge. A spell there, and then we come to Texas—"

"We," said Ramsey quickly. "Baton Rouge where you met Nora Stewart?"

Concho's eyes went strangely flat, his mocking grin vanished. "Me and th' Stewarts come from Baton Rouge to Big Bend," he said. "Yeah." He turned away, brusquely. "You better git on down the canyon."

Ramsey stared at the broad back for a moment. Then, wordlessly, he swung up on the gelding, leaving Concho, Gibson Girl, the rifle in the saddle scabbard and the glasses slung over the horn.

Nora Stewart was awake when Ramsey rode up. She had sponged the day's covering of dust off her face, had combed her hair, and she had a smokeless fire going, beans cooking and bacon sizzling. "Everything all right?" she asked Ramsey as he swung down.

"So far," he said.

"I thought I'd cook for us while it was still light. We won't dare risk a fire after dark."

Ramsey strode over to the fire. "Why don't you get some more rest? I'll take care of this."

She shook her head. "Cooking's woman's work. As long as I'm here, I'll take care of it. Besides . . . it's good for my nerves. It's . . . something ordinary, familiar." She shook her head. "Maybe you don't know what I mean."

"I reckon I do," Ramsey said. He accepted the cup of coffee she passed to him. "You've been through a lot this past couple of weeks, haven't you? I'm beginning to feel rotten about swinging you back out into the desert again."

"It doesn't matter," she said, crouched before the fire, not looking at him. "It's worth it if it'll help me pay off those lynchers from North Wells. Don't worry about me. I . . . I'm tougher than I look." She paused. "The main thing," she said presently, "is for you not to get yourself killed. You won't be any use to us in North Wells dead."

"I'm not going to get killed," said Ramsey. "But I'm going to get my horses back."

She stood up, hands on hips, and looked at him. "You are a stubborn man," she said.

"They're all I got."

She was silent for a moment. Then she said, questioningly, "A man as old as you? What about wife, family?"

Ramsey shook his head.

"Yes," she said, after a pause. "You'd have to be a lone wolf, wouldn't you? To start out on something like this with no help." She turned back to the fire and lifted bacon from the pan and spread it on a clean rock. "Why didn't you ride with that first, big bunch from North Wells? As far as that goes, if you go back there with us and take our part against them, won't you ruin yourself with those people?"

"I don't care about those people," Ramsey said, "and they don't care about me. Nobody back there would shed a tear if I didn't come out of this desert at all."

Slicing more bacon, she said, "That's a strange way to be —to live in a town like that for a long time and not have any friends."

Ramsey hesitated. He disliked talking about his personal affairs with anyone. And yet— Almost against his will, he found himself offering explanations.

"It's something that started years back," he said. "Right after the war." He meant the Civil War. "My dad was from Pennsylvania. He was just a kid when he joined the Union cavalry, toward the tail end of the fighting. But when the war was done with, he stayed in the Army. They sent him down here to Texas with the troops that occupied the South." Ramsey hesitated. "He was a lieutenant," he finished. "A white officer in an outfit that was all-Negro."

"Good heavens," Nora said with complete understanding. "A Yankee soldier in a Negro outfit? No wonder they hated him."

"They're still just as bitter today as they were then. Anyhow, he fell in love with this country—and with my mother. He took his discharge down here, bought some land, and settled down. He wanted to just mix in with the community; he liked these people—but, of course, they weren't about to have it." Ramsey's voice harshened. "When he married my mother, her family disowned her. They never spoke to her again as long as they lived."

"Oh, that must have been terrible," Nora said.

"It was," Ramsey said grimly. "If my old man'd had any sense, he would have given up and moved back North. But he was stubborn; he stayed on. But until the day my parents died, the people around North Wells treated 'em like lepers."

"And they treat you the same way?"

"I was born here," Sam Ramsey said. "I raise and train the best horses in this part of the country and I pay my bills on time. It's a little easier for me, but not much. These folks have got a long memory. I don't give a damn, though. I don't want any more to do with them then they want to do with me. When I was a boy growin' up, we learned to get along without 'em, to depend on ourselves. And I don't think I'll ever forgive 'em for the way they treated my mother—" He drank the rest of the coffee quickly, though it was scalding hot. "They go their way and I go mine, and we leave it like that."

"I see," Nora said.

Ramsey rolled a cigarette. "Anyhow," he said, "that's my story. What's yours? How'd you come to be on a desert ranch with your husband? This is a God-forsaken place for anybody to bring a woman to."

"I liked it here," she said. "Away from everybody. It's big and empty and . . . and clean. Or it was, until Sheep Kelly drifted in."

"Where are you from originally?"

She hesitated. Then she said, "I came here from Baton Rouge." As if to forestall further questioning, she suddenly became furiously busy at the fire. Then she turned, holding out a tin plate. "Here's your supper," she said.

He looked up at her. The freshening breeze whipped wisps of chestnut hair about her ears and molded shirt and leather skirt briefly to her body. She stood above him straight and proud and yet somehow vulnerable, a woman who could endure and yet remain a woman. Something stirred within him, something new and strange. He took the plate. "Thanks," he said. Now there were more questions than ever in his mind, but he knew she did not want to hear them and suddenly he realized that he did not want to ask them. He ate quickly and with complete preoccupation, and then he stood up. "That was good," he said. "I'll go send Concho back for his."

Twilight came to this country in an explosion of color—yellow, red, blue, purple. The immensity of the sky flamed, and sand and rock reflected it back; as light ebbed, soft and velvety shadows filled the space it left. As Concho and Ramsey packed the horses, the upper parts of the canyon rims blazed and glowed and then began to fade.

"Night travel's always best in this country," Concho said. "Leastways this time of year. Even if you ain't worried about somebody shootin' you." He finished his hitch and tucked the end of the rope under. "We oughta make Tornillo Creek by midnight. Then we go down to—" He broke off.

Ramsey pulled tight on a lash rope and looked up. Concho had stepped back from the animal, was standing very straight, tense, his head cocked on one side. His hand was on the butt of his gun. He looked like some giant wild beast tasting the air for any scent of enemy.

"What's wrong?" Ramsey asked, suddenly alarmed.

Concho made a silencing motion. Then Ramsey heard it, too. It was only a faint clink—steel against rock. But he recognized it—a shod horse coming. His hand swooped down and jerked his own Colt, and at the same instant, he and Concho both made protective moves toward Nora. Concho got there first, and his big hand pushed her down. "Take cover, honey," he rasped. To Ramsey: "Git that saddle gun. Somebody coming."

Ramsey wheeled toward Gibson Girl, reaching for the sheathed carbine. Then the laugh rang out above them.

It was bold, loud, mocking. And just as his hand hit the stock of the weapon it ended. A harsh voice shouted down. "Mister, touch that gun and you're dead!"

Ramsey froze, swiveling his head. Two hundred feet up, on the canyon's rim, he saw the silhouetted head and shoulders of a man sheltered behind an outcropping; and the dying light glinted off the barrel of a Springfield, pointed down toward them with a perfect field of fire.

"Concho!" the man yelled, as the Negro took a step toward the shelter of a horse. "Stand hitched."

Concho froze.

"This is Redfield," the voice went on. "You know I can shoot."

"Redfield?" Ramsey whispered.

"One of Sheep Kelly's men," Concho said bitterly. "God *damn!*"

"Now," Redfield called. "Both of you. Throw them sidearms down, easy. You're both big bastards, but this thing throws plenty of lead to cut you down to size." He gave that mocking laugh again.

"Awright, Redfield," Concho called back. "Hold yo' fire." And, with fingers carefully spread, he pulled the Colt from his pants and tossed it aside.

"You, too, Big Ugly," Redfield called.

Ramsey looked at Nora. She lay sprawled on the ground; her face was a strange color, chalk-white beneath its tan. She was, he realized, terrified. Ramsey grunted a curse, eased down the hammer on the Colt, and dropped it in the sand.

"Better," said Redfield, and now he yelled even louder. "Okay, boys, I got the drop!"

Immediately, the sound of horses became louder and open.

As Ramsey cautiously turned his head, two riders came around the canyon bend, the one in the rear leading a saddled horse. Ramsey sucked in a quick breath, recognizing the mounts as Morgans from his own herd.

The rider in the forefront swung down and passed his reins up to the man with the led horse. He was squat and beardy, and the straw skimmer he wore looked strange and out of place above his dust-covered face and his range clothes. Drawing a Colt .45 automatic from an army holster at his side, he came forward, but he stopped well clear of Concho.

A gap-toothed grin split his dusty beard. "Well, howdy, Concho. Miz Stewart. It sure is good to see y'all alive and well." His eyes swung to Ramsey. "And you—? I judge from your horses that it was your place we called on t'other night. Damn nice of you to bring the ones we missed in here to us."

Nora Stewart got to her feet. "What do you want with us, Lyman?"

Lyman bowed slightly and tipped his hat. "Well, ma'am, we seen where them people from up north burned your ranch and what they did to pore ole Hank. But we couldn't find no trace of you and Concho, so Sheep sent us out to look fer you."

"You go back and tell Sheep we're all right," she said commandingly.

Lyman's grin widened. " 'Fraid that wouldn't satisfy him. He give us orders to find you and bring you in. Concho, too, if he wants to come. And you know how Sheep is about orders. We wouldn't dare disobey 'em."

Concho, oblivious to the guns, took a step forward. "You ain't takin' nobody!" he snarled. "Sheep Kelly ain't puttin' his dirty hands on her!"

Lyman half-turned, raising the Colt, all semblance of good humor wiped from his face. "Listen, nigger, any more talk like that, I'll drop you where you stand. I don't like niggers that act around a white woman the way you do, nohow."

"You shut your damned mouth!" Concho roared, and suddenly he was an animal crouched to spring.

Nora Stewart screamed, a high, shattering sound that echoed in the canyon. Lyman pulled the automatic's trigger; as Concho launched himself, the gun thundered twice; Concho was snapped around by the impact of the bullets and fell sprawling in the sand. "Concho!" Nora screamed again and started toward him, but Lyman seized her wrist, jerked her around. She raked at him with clawed fingers, and blood welled from his face. *"Hold it!"* Redfield bellowed from above, as Ramsey was about to charge, and the Springfield went off, spraying sand in front of Ramsey. The other man

54

had sprung down off the horse by then; he seized Nora from behind and pinioned her arms. But she did not stop fighting; like a hellion, she spat and kicked ferociously; then Lyman, rubbing his bleeding face, stepped forward. His right hand moved, fist clubbed; her head snapped back and she went limp, knees buckling. Lyman let out a rasping breath and rubbed his face again. "Damn, what a panther!" he snapped. "Put her on a horse and tie her hands to th' horn."

The other man looked at Ramsey. "What about *this* joker?"

Lyman turned to face Ramsey. "Yeah, boy, what about you? Anybody else with you?"

Ramsey didn't answer. Lyman stepped forward, the automatic tilted to rake his face with the sight. "You by yourself?"

"Bound to be," Redfield called down. "When I got up here, I checked. Nobody in sight anywhere. No dust, no sign."

"We'll let *him* answer," Lyman snapped. "Well? You better talk when I ask you somethin'!"

Ramsey looked into the twisted, beardy face. "I'm alone," he said tersely.

Lyman's mouth curled. "And you come to git your horses back. All by yourself. Where'd you meet up with Concho and the woman?"

"Place called Double Springs," Ramsey said. "This morning."

"And they threw in with you?"

"They had to," Ramsey said. "I had the horses and the gear."

"Well, you ain't got 'em any longer," Lyman said. "We can use these Morgans and your goods, too. That includes the water." He unhooked a canteen from Gibson Girl's saddle and threw it to the ground at Ramsey's feet. "This much we leave you. If you're a good walker, you jest might make it back to North Wells. But I wouldn't wanta bet money on it."

"Whyn't you go ahead and plug 'im?" Redfield called down. "Or you want me to do it?"

Lyman flipped a hand. "Nope. Sheep wouldn't like it. The nigger don't make no difference, but killin' one of them North Wells ranchers is somethin' else. That might be just what it'd take to git the Army down in here. Let 'im walk out; if he makes it, fine. If he don't, nobody can pin it on us; it was the desert."

Redfield spat all the way down into the canyon. "You're gittin' so you sound jest like Sheep."

"Sheep uses his head. And you know his orders—no unnecessary killin'." Lyman grinned. "By the way, *hombre*—

55

thanks for flashin' signals to us with them field glasses of yours. Sun on the lenses shines a long way off, and we never woulda found you if it hadn't been for that." He backed to his horse and then swung up. "Reddy, you kin come down, now. We got to ride." Nora Stewart was a limp bundle in Gibson Girl's saddle, and the other man steadied her. Lyman gathered all of Ramsey's animals into a string. *"Adios, hombre."* His voice was mocking. *"Bueno suerte!"* Then, in darkness, the cavalcade moved out of the canyon, and except for the body of Concho, Ramsey was alone.

He stood motionless, until the sound of hooves on rock had faded. Then the paralysis that held him broke, and he began to curse his own stupidity. If only he'd shielded the lenses of the binoculars . . .

But the damage was done, now, completely, beyond repair. His horses were gone forever. But somehow that didn't matter. What mattered was that Nora Stewart was gone, too, that she—

Savagely, he made himself stop thinking. He went to Concho and wrestled the sprawled body over. The front of the Negro's shirt was a sticky mess of blood and sand. Ramsey touched it and drew his hand away. Then he tensed.

He put his hand back. Concho's body was still very warm. And as Ramsey groped toward the wound, from Concho's clenched teeth came a long rasping breath. Sam Ramsey stared down at the Negro and shook his head. Though he did now know whether to be relieved, or appalled at the extra burden this laid upon him, at least for now Concho still lived.

★ CHAPTER SEVEN ★

Sunlight awakened Sam Ramsey.

He sat up, blinking, cold, cramped, disoriented. Rubbing beardy face and gritty eyes, he could not remember for a moment where he was or what had happened. Then recollection came to him, bitterly, and he got stiffly to his feet and looked down at Concho, who was snoring raspingly, his skin curiously ashen. The bandage Ramsey had made from his undershirt was blood-soaked, but the blood was dried; apparently the bleeding had stopped.

Last night, in darkness, he had not been able to tell how badly Concho was hit. But they had left him matches and he had kindled a blaze; in its light, he cut away the sandy mess of the shirt. What was revealed was a bloody mass of chopped meat, and it took careful probing to ascertain what had happened.

Concho had been lucky. The heavy slug, adopted only a few years before by the Army because a .38 would not stop a *jurimentado* Moro, had slammed into Concho's flank, shattered a rib—there were bone splinters in the wound—and, glancing, had keyholed out, making a terrible exit hole. The second shot, almost instantaneous with the first, had almost missed; it had only chopped up more of the flesh on Concho's flank. Apparently no vital organs had been damaged; but shock and loss of blood had kept Concho out all night.

There had been nothing Ramsey could do for him but make a huge poultice of creosote leaves moistened with a little of his precious water and strap it in place with his undershirt. Still, barring infection, the chances were good that Concho would not die of his wounds.

Which, Ramsey had reflected last night, did not make things a bit easier for him now. There was no food and not enough water for him to remain here in the canyon with Concho even a single night, if he were to survive. It was fifteen miles back to the springs where they had met yesterday, and it was either make that march tonight or risk not making it at all.

For the logistics of the problem were simple. There was still water in his body and perhaps a quart and a half in the gallon canteen. If he started now, he would be in fairly good shape when he reached the springs. If he did not, it would be tomorrow night before he could travel, for there was no hope of making it in the furnace-like heat of day. And by tomorrow night, his body would be dehydrated and his supply of water reduced; by then, he probably could not make the springs at all.

Goddammit, he thought, this is a man who has already tried to kill me once. If the situation was reversed, he wouldn't think twice about leaving me and saving himself. There ain't enough water to save him anyway; he's lost too much blood and it would take all there is in this canteen and more to replace it. I don't owe him anything—why let him drag me down with him?

The more he thought about it, the more plainly the odds were written. If he went ahead now, he could survive. If he waited, they both were dead. Besides, he owed it to Nora Stewart to make the try. If he could reach North Wells, he vowed savagely, he'd take the first train to El Paso, and if the army commandant there wouldn't mount an expedition against Sheep Kelly, he'd strangle the soldier with his bare hands . . .

"Yes, by God!" he had said aloud, in final resolve; and then he sprang to his feet and seized the canteen and slung it over his shoulder. Moving cautiously in the almost total darkness beyond the range of the fire, he had started towards the northern outlet of the canyon. Fifty feet he made, before he halted.

There was no reason for him to stop. Behind him, the fire was blazing with the fresh wood he'd piled on it; Concho lay beside it, inert and silent. Ramsey stood there a moment, said, "Hell," and moved on.

But not far. Once more he halted, turned, and glanced back at the circle of firelight. Then he looked forward. Another ten paces and he would be around a corner of the canyon wall. Then he would be able to see neither the fire nor Concho. Hitching at the canteen decisively, he started again.

This time, he made it around that corner. Now the way lay clear before him; he could see where the canyon widened. Stars rode the sky in an incredible profusion of constellations. Soon the sliver of moon would come up. There would not be much light, but there would be enough to walk by. He strode on.

He reached the end of the canyon. Now, ahead of him, the desert floor lay open. The walking would be easier; following their backtrail, he calculated that he could make the springs in seven hours, well before sunrise. He could fill the canteen there—with careful nursing, a gallon of water should carry him through two more nights' march, thirty, forty miles, if his feet did not give out in these high-heeled boots. That would put him well within ranching country and range of help.

It was a delicate equation, and it would have to balance exactly, everything would have to go just right, but he could make it. All he had to do was keep going and he would live. Of course, by tomorrow night Concho would be dead. But that couldn't be helped. Hell, he thought, if the bullet had hit only an inch or two farther to the left, the Negro would have been killed immediately anyhow. He was not Concho's murderer; Lyman was. Ramsey hitched at the canteen and began to walk again. He made a hundred feet, and then he said an obscenity, loudly and bitterly, for it was not going to work, and he knew it. It was just not going to work.

And he turned around, still cursing himself for a fool, and made his way once more into the canyon. When he reached the place where Concho lay, the Negro had not moved and the fire had burned down to coals.

Through the night, Ramsey sat beside the black man. He sat there and smoked too much of his remaining tobacco and wasted too much water sponging off the sweaty, contorted face of Concho. He was careful not to think any more.

Not too long before dawn, Concho began to toss and roll; and then he began to mumble, the profane, disconnected babble of delirium. But as it went on and on, it began to form a pattern; Ramsey began to see the outline of a hard, combative, desperate life. *Man, you say that again, I cut your throat . . . Mama? Mama? Where you gone, Mama? Listen, boys, the lieutenant say we got to go up yonder after that there blockhouse . . . Set that Gatlin' gun up over here, we kin sweep ever'thing down yonder, them Mescans come again . . . He didn't hurt me; I take him next round sure . . .*

There was a lot of that, but it was not what bothered Ramsey. What brought him upright, listening carefully, was the way Nora's name suddenly began to weave in and out of Concho's delirium.

Now you look here, Miss Annie. That girl different from these other sluts in this house . . . Nora, we got to git you outa here . . . Stewart, you don't take her without you take me. Ain't no man have her without I watch him close . . . You don't treat her good, I'll be on hand to kill you . . . Run, Nora, run . . . Don't worry, honey, I'll see they git what's comin' to 'em . . . No, I don't dare. Oh, God, I want to, but I don't dare . . . Noracita. My little Noracita . . .

Concho's purplish lips writhed back from yellow teeth; his big body twisted, arched as if in agony.

"Oh, God, why you make her white and me black?"

Then he sank down, motionless, panting.

Ramsey got up and put more wood on the fire.

But after that, Concho was still. Presently Ramsey stretched out and tried to sleep, but, tired as he was, it was a long time before he sank into unconsciousness.

Now, satisfied that the bleeding had stopped, Ramsey poured a few drops of water onto his neckerchief and mopped sand and sweat from Concho's face. He was startled when the eyes opened wide and looked at him blankly, then focused and became rational.

Suddenly Concho tried to rise. *"Nora!"* he yelled. *"Where Nora?"*

Ramsey pushed him back. "Lyman took her with him to Sheep Kelly."

"We got to—" Concho forced himself up on his elbows, groaned, and dropped back. "Remember now," he husked. "How bad I hit?"

"Bad enough," Ramsey said. He told Concho what his wounds were.

Concho lay panting, staring at the sky. Then he mumbled, "I had worse, it never stopped me. Git th' horses, we got to go after her."

"They took the horses," Ramsey said flatly. "They took all the gear. We got nothing but a quart of water."

"And how much time . . . ? How much start they got?"

"A whole night," Ramsey said.

"A night? And you let me lay here—? We oughta . . . naw. Naw, you right. Wasn't nothin' you could do." He let out a rasping breath. Then he said, "I'm all right now. We got to start out after 'em. Don't try to stop me, I'm gittin' up."

Ramsey said, bluntly: "You start the bleedin' again, you're a dead man. We ain't got enough water to replace what you already lost."

Concho's bloodshot eyes glared at him. "Man, ain't you got no sense? Sheep Kelly's got that woman! And you want me to lay here?"

Ramsey said, "Suit yourself." He backed away.

Concho began to struggle to his feet. His black face went gray with agony as he pushed his torso up into a sitting position. He sucked in his lower lip and bit it, and Ramsey could hear the loud rasp of his breathing. Ramsey watched the bandage closely, but there was no fresh blood so far.

Sitting, Concho paused for breath and strength. Then he uttered an explosive curse of self-disgust and in one mighty effort somehow was on his feet. He stood there panting and swaying and leaned against the canyon wall.

"God," he said, "sho am dizzy."

Ramsey held out the canteen. "You'd better take a drink."

Concho stared at it. "Only a quart, you say?"

"Maybe less."

Concho's tongue licked his lips. Then he said, "Later. I don't need no water now." He rubbed his face with the palm of a hand, moping away the oily sweat his efforts had brought to it. Still there was no fresh, red stain on his bandage. "We ain't got no time to lose," he said. "We got to start out after her."

"Don't be a fool," Ramsey said. "You're in no shape to go anywhere. We'll wait 'til night; then, if you can walk at all, we'll head back for Double Springs. We'll stay there until you're well enough to go on."

"No," Concho snapped. What flared in his eyes as he looked at Ramsey could have been fever-glow or a kind of insanity, or both. "Man, you don't know that Sheep Kelly.

60

He the lowest of the low—I seen Mex girls he had. When it come to women, he just like a damn animal, worse . . . You think I'm gonna leave Nora—" He hitched himself up, drew in a deep breath, and winced at the pain of it. "Come on. We gotta go."

The sun was high now, clear of the canyon walls. Ramsey gestured toward its round, white dazzle. "With a quart of water . . . in that? And you shot up?"

"We git water," Concho said.

"Where?"

Concho gestured vaguely. "There water out there, I know where. We find it all right."

"No," Ramsey said. He picked up the canteen, slung it over his shoulder and held its strap in a tight grip.

Concho looked at him and the canteen with hatred. Then he said hoarsely, "Awright. You go where you want to. I goin' after Nora." He turned his face from Ramsey and began to walk.

It was a travesty of a walk, a swaying, lurching, tortuous, loose-jointed process of lifting one foot with the utmost effort, then the other; and even as he did it, Concho had to brace himself on the wall of the canyon with a hand. Ramsey stood motionless and watched him. Concho could not keep that up longer than a minute or two; then he would collapse. Ramsey thought: It's hopeless. I should have gone on last night.

And yet, amazingly, Concho refused to fall. Five steps, ten, twenty. Ramsey could hear him panting and see the sweat on his head and neck and his naked torso where it showed through the rags of the shirt and the bandage. But instead of weakening with each step, he seemed to be gaining strength, and suddenly, with a decisive gesture, he pushed himself away from the canyon wall and shambled slowly on without support. He stumbled down into the dry stream-bed that ran through the canyon, and Ramsey heard him grunt. But he did not fall. Swaying, lurching, he kept on, lifting first one foot and then the other and planting them carefully in the sand of the wash.

Now, without even looking back at Ramsey, he was about to round the turn. Ramsey stood there frozen for a moment longer; then, hardly realizing what he was about, he ran after Concho.

"All right," he said when he caught up with Concho. "Damn it, all right."

Concho said, without looking around, "You coming?"

Ramsey took Concho's arm. "You better lean on me," he

said. Then he said, "You better not be lying about the water. If we don't find it, we'll both be dead by tomorrow night."

"We find it somewhere," Concho mumbled. He shook off Ramsey's grasp. "I kin walk by myself," he said.

Ramsey stared at the glittering wasteland ahead of them. As well die, he thought, going in one direction as another; and slowly he and Concho left the canyon and marched on into the merciless sunlight.

It was not long before Concho, despite his protestations, needed Ramsey's help. As they crossed a flat strewn with rock and gravel, bristled with yucca and cholla and prickly pear, Concho swayed and would have fallen into a tangle of cactus if Ramsey had not caught him. With an effort, as Ramsey steadied him, Concho stiffened his buckling legs, clinging to Ramsey with his right arm about the other's shoulders. Concho's breath was hot and foul in Ramsey's face, and Concho's eyes were half-glazed. But the Negro muttered savagely, "I all right."

"Like hell," Ramsey croaked. He had not allowed himself any water, either, and his lips were swollen and split. His mouth felt as if it and his throat were clogged with dust. In addition, the high-heeled boots, never made for walking, had already rubbed his heels raw. He blinked into the glare of a cloudless sky and then dragged Concho to the dubious shade of a small boulder. Its shadow covered only their heads, as they sprawled on their backs. Ramsey unplugged the canteen. "You'd better take a drink," he gasped, passing it to Concho.

The Negro did not protest, as Ramsey had expected. He put the neck of the canteen to his mouth and took two cautious swallows. Ramsey found himself watching closely, jealously, greedily, to make sure Concho did not drink too much. Then he wiped the canteen's neck and took a single swallow himself, letting the tepid water sluice deliciously around his dry mouth before he swallowed it.

Closing the canteen, he also closed his eyes. "We'll never make it," he said, "unless the next water's close. Where is it?"

After a very long moment, Concho husked: "I think there some at a place called Cartridge Springs."

"You *think?* You *think?*" Ramsey hoisted himself on one elbow.

"It run dry sometime. Not very often."

"How far?"

Concho lay with eyes closed. "Ten miles," he said. "Maybe twelve." He paused as if gathering strength to talk. Then he pointed toward a mountain rearing above broken country across a huge expanse of heat-shimmering, gently rising flat. "Yonder. Foot of Rosillo Mountain."

Ramsey stared despairingly at the jumble of peak and ridge and arroyo. "Christ," he whispered. "We'll never make it, shape you're in."

"We'll make it," Concho rasped. "Drink good, fill the canteen, then we wait for night, head on down Tornillo Creek to Chilicotal. That where your horses are; Sheep Kelly and Nora be there, too. Don't worry, we make it somehow." He touched the wound on his side. "Anyhow, it ain't bleedin'. And if it ain't started up by now, it ain't goin' to."

Ramsey said, "You got a shattered rib in there. It must be givin' you hell."

"I can stand it," Concho said. After a moment, he said, "I can stand anything I got to stand. You want to help me up? Layin' here ain't gettin' us no closer to Cartridge Springs."

The rest of that day was as much delirium for Sam Ramsey as it must have been for the tortured Concho. It turned out that when the Negro was on his feet, try as he would, he could not walk without bracing himself against Ramsey. But with his arm around Ramsey's shoulder, he could make stumbling progress. That was the way they traveled.

By noon, they had made perhaps three miles, maybe four, and they were both exhausted. The sun was like a hammer pounding at them fiercely and without cessation. The heat sucked the water out of their bodies greedily, but their shirts never became wet; evaporation and the occasional dust-swirling furnace wind that blew dried all wetness immediately.

Rosillo Mountain seemed no closer than it had been hours before. Ramsey's stomach was beginning to growl with hunger, but thirst was, of course, the real torment. Next to the thirst, hunger and even the pain of his raw-rubbed feet shrank to minor inconveniences. It was the first time he could remember that his whole body had been thirsty. He wanted not only to drink water, but to plunge into it, wallow in it, let gallons of it soak in through his pores.

Instead, inexorably, it oozed out. What they allowed themselves from the canteen replaced not one twentieth of what they lost through perspiration. Ramsey's very eyeballs felt dry and harsh.

They nooned in the scant shade of two yuccas growing fortuitously close together and five feet tall. They did not dare wait too long, though: Now they were in a race with complete dehydration. When whatever scanty water remained in their bodies was gone, they would not be able to travel at all. And Cartridge Springs was a lifetime away. Seven miles, maybe eight, Concho said. Alone, even with his raw feet, Ramsey could have made it in three hours, anyhow. But Concho's weakness slowed their pace to half the normal walking speed of even a weary man, and the exertion of supporting the big Negro's body sapped Ramsey of his own strength and made his fatigue far deeper than it should have been by now.

They arose and went on. Presently they crossed the wind-blown ruts that comprised all the road there was into this part of Big Bend; by the road, said Concho, it was twice or maybe three times again as far to water at this time of year. They left the road and inched on toward the blue mountains, so near and yet so far away; and now the country was becoming rougher and more broken; there were deep arroyos to circle and draws to climb, their graveled bottoms and sides treacherous footing. Ramsey lost track of time; all he knew was that the sun, the damnable sun, was drying and shriveling him like a prune, and that if there were not water in Cartridge Springs, they were finished. By this time tomorrow, if not dead, they would no longer be conscious.

They wasted no breath on talking. But once, in midafternoon, Concho's voice, seemingly from far away, impinged on Ramsey's mind. "It ain't hurtin' so much. My side. It ain't hurtin' near as much."

Ramsey had no strength left to answer. But he thought vaguely that Concho was probably growing numb and faint, and that was why the pain was less.

Somehow it had become late afternoon. The sun, down-slanting, was still hot and terrible, but less so than before. The mountain loomed ahead of them now, peak and hogback and hump; and it was changing color. They stumbled across a dry-wash, and then Ramsey's grip on Concho's arm tightened. "Look," he whispered, unable to speak aloud. "That's it, ain't it? Ain't that it?"

Ahead, in a draw at the foot of the mountain, there was a faint mist of greenery. It made startling contrast to the brown and red of rock, the drab hues of creosote and cactus. Cottonwood and willow brush, Ramsey thought, hope rising in him and strengthening him almost like water itself. "Oh, God," he said, "that's gotta be it. Come on, Concho—!"

But the Negro neither answered nor quickened his pace. Ramsey turned his head, stared at the black face six inches above his own. It was ashen, the cheeks were sunken, and there was no more sweat on Concho's skin. "Concho," Ramsey said hoarsely.

Although his feet moved on, in their slow, uncertain rhythm, Concho gave no sign of hearing. Ramsey used his other hand to catch Concho's chin, turn the face around.

Then he gasped. The eyes were sunken in the skull, glazed and unfocused. An eerie chill went up Ramsey's spine. This man was dying—and yet he did not, would not, stop walking.

A half mile, Ramsey thought. Surely the spring could be no more than a half mile. He halted; when he did, Concho's feet kept moving. But Ramsey slid out from under the long, ropy arm and then he caught the lanky, rawboned body as it collapsed.

As gently as he could, he lowered Concho to the ground. The Negro lay on his back, eyes open, staring at the sun. His chest rose and fell with his shallow breathing. Ramsey looked at the bandage. There was a small but growing spot of fresh, vivid red on its dirty surface.

Ramsey pulled Concho's sombrero over the Negro's eyes. Then he unslung the canteen and shook it. Three, perhaps four swallows of water, carefully hoarded, left in it. He unplugged it, took one small swallow that was more delicious than anything he had ever tasted in his life. When he had at last allowed it to trickle down his throat, he felt sad. If there were not water over there, if the spring had died, only its last faint moisture keeping the greenery alive, this would be the last drink he would ever take.

Then he raised Concho's head and carefully poured the rest of the canteen's pathetic burden into Concho's mouth.

It was not enough to revive the Negro. But perhaps it would keep him alive until he, Ramsey, could get back from the spring. Ramsey got uncertainly to his feet, slung the canteen once again, and, feeling strengthened by relief from Concho's weight, hobbled on burning feet toward where the spring should be.

Truly enough, he saw, as he reached the mouth of a narrow draw, there was a clump of willow and cottonwood. Suddenly, too, there was grunting and snorting and the clatter of little hooves on gravel and from the bushes exploded a half-dozen javelinas, the little wild pigs of the desert, bristles erect, tusks gleaming. As Ramsey shrank to one side, they scuttled down the draw, poured past him so close he could catch their rank and musky odor, and then were gone. His heart pounding from the sudden fright and from hope and yearning and desperation, Ramsey stumbled on up the draw. At last he reached the screen of brush, parted it, and forced his way through.

The pigs had muddied the water; but it was there, a gallon or two in a shallow rock tank hollowed over the years by the slow seepage from a face of solid rock. What overflow there was traveled not a yard before it was totally lost in dry sand. Ramsey crashed down in the brush until he was lying flat, and then he buried his face in the tepid, foul, and blessed liquid.

It was nearly a half hour later before he got back to Concho. It had taken that long for his own strength to revive. The Negro lay on the desert, exactly as Ramsey had left him. The red stain on the bandage was much bigger now. For a moment, Ramsey could detect no motion of Concho's chest or belly and was sure the Negro was dead. But when he put his hand over Concho's heart, he could feel a faint but surprisingly steady rhythm.

Ramsey got the Negro's head up on his own knees. When he took off the sombrero, Concho's eyes were still open, dull and vacuous. Ramsey put the canteen to Concho's mouth, let water seep slowly in, trying to be careful not to strangle the man. When a half pint had disappeared, Ramsey poured perhaps a quart over Concho's face. Then he gave Concho another drink and sat down, himself exhausted once again, and lit a cigarette.

Presently Concho's chest moved with a deep breath, and Concho said gently, almost absently: "Nora?"

"Wake up, Concho," Ramsey said.

Concho blinked. "Who that?"

"Ramsey."

"Oh." Concho at last closed his eyes. Then he said, "I ain't thirsty no more." His voice was a whisper. "We at the spring?"

"Almost," Ramsey said. "It's a half mile over yonder."

Concho lay quietly and in silence for perhaps three minutes. Then he said: "Gimme a hand up. I can make it."

★ CHAPTER EIGHT ★

The damnable thing about the desert, Sam Ramsey thought, was the way it could fry you all day and freeze you all night. Now that the sun had gone down, it was bitterly cold at the springs. The wind that swept across the flats without hindrance almost had a touch of ice in it; they were, after all, at an altitude of nearly three thousand feet here.

Yet, they did not dare risk a fire. The temperature would not drop low enough to threaten them, not if they kept to the shelter of the draw, which broke the worst impact of the wind. Here, in darkness, nagged by hunger, they lay sprawled as best they could arrange themselves on gravel and rock. Ramsey had rebandaged Concho's wounds, and the seepage of blood had apparently stopped. Despite the chill, Concho had fallen asleep almost immediately, and he had slept nearly without moving, a deep, drugged slumber. Now he had awakened, and Ramsey who had slept only fitfully, heard him drinking from the canteen.

Ramsey sat up, lit a cigarette, and had a drink himself. Overhead, the sky was salted with stars. Occasionally, down the draw, there was a startled snort, as one of the deer flocking to the spring caught their scent and retreated. Ramsey said, "How you feeling?"

"Better," Concho said. "A whole lot better. I be ready to travel again tomorrow."

"We aren't traveling tomorrow," Ramsey said.

"The hell you say!" Concho snapped. Ramsey heard the clatter of gravel as Concho, groaning slightly, propped himself up on his elbow. "I tell you I'm all right. And I ain't gonna let Kelly—"

Ramsey said, coldly, cruelly: "Whatever Kelly wants to do to her, he's already done by now."

Concho's indragged breath made a shuddering sound in the night.

Then Ramsey went on, still in that cold tone. "It shouldn't make much difference anyhow, considering the place Stewart married her out of."

Concho said in a strangled voice, "Goddam you—"

"So why would it matter to her?" Ramsey said. Then his voice went on, brutally beating at Concho. "I dragged you here, by God. Another mile and you'd have never made it, you'd be dead by now, and maybe me with you. Those holes in your side have got to have time to heal. You may be big and tough, but you ain't made out of iron. The way it is now, we could walk up on Kelly and his outfit tomorrow, and after we'd made a day like today, they wouldn't even have to shoot us. They could knock us over with feathers. Long as you're in the shape you're in, you ain't worth a damn to yourself or me or her, either one. And neither am I as long as I got to drag you."

"You won't hafta drag me," Concho said ferociously.

"You think that now. It'll be another matter, noon tomorrow." Ramsey's voice was flat. "You go on, you go by yourself. I don't aim to be bothered with you any more. Not until you're strong enough to take care of yourself and pay your own way."

There was silence. Then Concho's voice said, subtly, "Your

hawses are at Chilicotal Springs right now. We wait, they'll be across the Rio, another coupla days."

"I'm not thinking of my horses," Ramsey said; and he was surprised to find that it was true. He paused a moment, examining that in his own mind before he went on. "I'm thinking about Nora Stewart."

"After what you said about her—"

"It's true, ain't it?"

Silence. Then Concho letting out a gusty breath. "Yeah," he said. "It's true." His voice quickened; there was urgency in it, almost pleading. "But you got to understand about it. She was not like any of the other girls. She a lady—"

"Sure," said Ramsey.

"She born a lady," Concho said. "She come from a good family in Baltimore, only . . . she got mixed up with a worthless no-account man when she not really old enough to know better. Her family come between 'em and she ran off with him." His voice harshened with hatred, bitterness, a score long unpaid. "When he tired of her, he run off and leave her in Baton Rouge. She don't know how to do nothing to earn a living and she don't dare go home and . . . Miss Annie's a high-class place. It a lot better than starving."

"That's where you met her?"

Concho's voice was soft. "Yeah. That where I met her. I work for Miss Annie, tend bar, bouncer, I see right away Miss Nora ain't no ordinary hog-ranch girl. I . . . I make it my business try to watch over her best I can.

"Then Hank Stewart come along. He fall for her and ask her to marry him. She say it wouldn't be fair to him. I tell her, he know what he is doing. Then she say, it still wouldn't be fair, she didn't love him. She say she don't think she ever gonna love any man again in her whole life." His voice tapered off. Ramsey could hear his breathing in the darkness. "But I make her see at last it her only chance. She go ahead and marry him and he bring her here. He not the best man in the world, but he not a bad 'un, either. And she . . . she got thoroughbred blood in her, all right. Ain't no man could ask for a better wife than she made him."

Ramsey ground out the cigarette. "How come Sheep Kelly didn't take her from Stewart long time ago? If he wanted her, with all the men he had . . ."

"He needed Stewart," Concho said. "Stewart never rustled with Sheep, never got any of the money, anything like that. But he had to buy the right to ranch in Kelly's territory, the right not to have Kelly bother his wife or his stock. He did it by freightin' in supplies to Kelly, lettin' him use the place for a waystation for rustled cows now and again, keepin' his ear to the ground and pickin' up news . . . He didn't like it, but he had to do it to keep his wife and goods and stay alive." A match flared as Concho lit a cigarette of his own. Then his voice roughened. "How'd you know where she come from?"

"You talked a lot last night after you was shot."

Concho swore.

"Another reason we ain't startin' out tomorrow," Ramsey went on inexorably, "is that we got to make a plan. The two of us can't take on all of Kelly's bunch single-handed."

Concho said thinly, "You was aimin' to do it to get your horses back."

"I had guns, then, too," Ramsey replied wryly. "And horses and supplies. And I didn't have any shot-up, played-out cow-hand hangin' around my neck. Things are a little bit different now. We got to git some guns and some mounts and some grub from somewhere before we can even think about takin' on Kelly. Ain't there some other ranches down in here?"

"If we go near 'em, we'll be cooked," Concho said bluntly. "They all tied in with Sheep just like Stewart was."

"Yeah, but suppose we could steal what we need from 'em."

Concho considered. Then he said, "No. We'd never make it. They keep too good an eye out. Part of the agreement of their workin' with Sheep is that he makes the Mescans lay off 'em, too. But these *Revolucionarios* gittin' more and more feisty. Especially after Vera Cruz, they liable to break out against the gringos down here, Sheep or no Sheep. Everybody down here's just about on a war footin' now. Stewart and me was like that, we kept watch all the time. But he wasn't afraid of that bunch from North Wells, that's where he made his mistake. He didn't know how mean and mad they was after gettin' shot up by the Mexes."

"Well, we got to figure out somethin'," Ramsey said.

Concho was quiet for a while. Then he said, "Goddammit."

Something in his tone brought Ramsey's head around. "What?"

"Stewart's place. They burned ever'thing. But the cave's still there."

"What cave?"

"Back up behind the ranch house, not far. When we got to worryin' about the Mescans, me and him started fixin' it up. We figured we might need a place to run to, kinda storm cellar, you know? If the *Revolucionarios* hit us, me and him and Nora could hole up there, let 'em raid the damn place, but at least we'd be safe. And if they found us, it made a fine fort;

it'd cost 'em more than they'd want to pay to dig us outa there. I shoulda thought of it before."

"What's in it?"

"Grub, anyhow. Plenty of that. And some rifles and ammo. Yes, by God. Two Springfields and plenty of ammo." His cigarette made a winking arc as he threw it away. "Me and Nora didn't dare go near the place once we got away. We was blocked off from the cave and had to hightail it in the other direction. And even after them bastards from North Wells left, I knew the smoke they made would draw Sheep and maybe the Mescans, too, to find out what was goin' on. I didn't dare bump into either one, they'da killed me outa hand and taken Nora."

"So there's still guns there and food. You sure?"

"Why wouldn't there be? Nobody's likely to of found it. You can't hardly see it, 'less you know where it is."

"How far is it?"

"South of Chilicotal Springs. A good forty miles from here, right between Talley Mountain and Chilicotal Mountain."

Ramsey thought of his own raw feet and Concho's weakness. "Will there be water between here and there?"

"We should be able to make Neville Spring all right. There's water at Dugout Wells, but we'll have to swing clear of that—too close to Chilicotal."

"Forty miles," Ramsey murmured. "We ought to make it in two nights, two and a half at most."

"Three or maybe four," Concho said. "We got to go through a lot of rough country. We make ten miles a night, we'll be doin' good." His voice roughened. "Thass why I say we got to go right away. If we don't, Sheep Kelly'll have had Nora for God knows how long before we catch up with 'im." Ramsey sensed the terror in the man—not for himself, but for the woman. "And—a man that's sick in his head about women, like Sheep . . . it don't take him long to . . . to use up a woman. 'Specially if she fight back."

"You think Nora will fight back?"

Concho was silent for a moment; when he spoke, there was misery in his voice. "I don't know," he said at last.

Ramsey sat there for a while, listening to the slow drip of the water and trying to think, to plan. But he kept seeing the woman's image in his mind: face, body, the graceful way she moved, and he heard her husky voice, and there was an urgency in him every bit as great as Concho's.

"When he git through with her," Concho said thinly, "he pass her on down to his men. When they finished, they turn her over to the Mescans. And after that—God knows what happen to her or where she wind up . . ."

70

A gust of cold wind came up the draw and Sam Ramsey shivered. But then he said quietly: "It can't be helped. You got to rest and heal up. We'll travel by night and day, too, to make up for lost time, if we can come by enough water and somethin' to eat. But I can't carry you from here to Stewart's place, and I can't do anything down in this country by myself against those people. We got to spend at least a day here, and maybe two if that's what it takes."

For a while, there was silence in the draw. Then Concho said, "Awright. If that's the way it got to be, it'll be that way."

* * *

Concho knew survival in the desert. "We fill our canteen, move away from this spring in daylight. This the only water for miles, anybody comin' through gonna stop here. We wanta be damn sure we see them 'fore they see us. 'Sides, we got to find ourselves somethin' to eat."

"Like what?" Ramsey asked.

Concho's lips curled wryly. "Like sidewinder," he said.

Ramsey's stomach convulsed at the thought. But hunger was a torment, and Concho was inexorable. They found a sheltered spot on a bench farther up the mountain, from which they could overlook the territory for miles, and Ramsey went out to look for snakes. He was not notably successful; rattlers were vulnerable to the intense heat and holed up during the day. But he managed to catch a couple, and under Concho's direction, he beheaded, skinned, and fileted them. Despite his hunger, it took some doing to force down the soft white meat, even when it had been roasted in the coals of a smokeless fire of brushwood.

"We got to have more'n that," Concho said, "if we gonna make Stewart's place. You know how to build a deadfall?"

"No," Ramsey said.

"If the coast clear, I show you this evenin' late," Concho said. "You have to do the work, though. There a lot of heavy liftin', and I might open this here wound."

A couple of hours before dark, Concho surveyed the country and seemed satisfied. "I reckon it all right to work down in the draw for a little while." With Ramsey's help, he and Ramsey climbed down off the bench.

"I been watchin' all day," Concho said. "We scared away all the game last night and they ain't come back to drink, yet. But they got to come sooner or later, because there ain't no other place to water. We'll put our trap here where the draw narrows down."

71

The worst part of it was finding the necessary wood. Ramsey had to climb back up the mountain until he could cut the pieces needed for triggers off some stunted junipers and piñons that grew at higher altitudes. Then, under Concho's directions, he bridged the draw with rock deadfalls at its narrowest point. First, a heavy upright stick to support a broad, flat stone upon which other stones were to be piled to increase the weight. Then a figure-four trigger contrivance, so that anything that hit it would bring the rock down crushingly. It took five of them to close the floor of the draw, and then there were stones to be piled on the sloping sides of the defile to make the barrier more complete.

"What we likely to git," Concho said, "is a javelina, if we lucky. They ain't drunk since yesterday evenin'. Tonight there may be some thirsty enough to come up here regardless of all the man scent we done left around here. The ones behind crowd the ones in front to git to water, if it a herd of any size, and maybe one of 'em git pushed or bump into them trap triggers. Then again, maybe we only git a jack rabbit or maybe we git nothin'. We move back up on the bench and wait and see."

Ramsey was too exhausted to reply. It took the last of his strength to help Concho back up the mountain. There they wolfed the last few crumbs of snake meat and huddled behind boulders that broke the chill wind of the desert night.

"We got to be very quiet tonight," Concho said. After a pause, he added: "I feelin' lots better, though. A good square meal and I sure I be ready to move on tomorrow night."

Ramsey didn't reply, and they lay in silence, shivering with the cold. Stars appeared in unbelievable profusion overhead, and a larger slice of moon came up. The night dragged on, endlessly. At last Ramsey slept.

He was jerked awake, heart pounding, by a hideous noise. It was a banshee shriek, rising from the draw, and it kept on and on and on, shrill, piercing, full of agony. He rubbed his eyes. "What the hell—?"

Concho's voice came from darkness, full of exultancy. "We got one. A javelina done tripped the trigger and he pinned down."

Ramsey comprehended then and sprang to his feet, but Concho caught his ankle. "Wait," the Negro rapped. "Them pigs is still down there in the draw. You go down there in the dark, they all excited, they cut you to ribbons. Jest wait."

Ramsey sank back down. The squealing went on for a long time. Then it died to a thin, rasping, pathetic sound. At last, Concho said, "You better go down now. But be careful. Herd

72

of javelinas can tear a man plumb apart with them tushes of theirs, they git riled. I think they gone, but you look out. And not only for them pigs. That's jest the kind of noise brings a cougar, and one of 'em might jump you thinkin' you were a deer."

Ramsey said nothing, but he pulled out his sheath knife and edged down off the bench. It took him a long time to make his way through darkness to the draw. By the time he reached it, he was tense and jumpy. But he found it empty, except for thirty pounds of young javelina, its hindquarters pinned under one of the collapsed piles of rock. There was still some life in it, and it gnashed its tusks at him as he stuck it with the blade.

At last he wrestled the carcass back up to the bench. "God," he said, as he dropped it on the rock. "This thing stinks like a skunk."

"It won't be no tender steak," Concho said wryly. "Lemme have your knife. I cut them musk glands out, it be better. Anyhow, we got us meat now. We cook it dry, it'll keep a coupla days. Wish to hell we could smoke it, but we don't dare."

The next morning, they built a fire and ate ravenously of the rank, stringy flesh. Concho cooked the rest of the meat until it was black and charred and there was no grease left in it. Then he divided it into two parts and shoved one toward Ramsey. "Stick that in yo' shirt," he commanded. "Soon as the worst of the heat's gone, we strike out."

Ramsey looked at him. "You feel good enough?"

"I'm fine," Concho said.

"You're lying in your teeth," Ramsey said. "That rib must be like a knife goin' through you every time you move."

Concho's eyes flared. "Goddammit, man, you think I got time for a rest cure or somethin'? We got to git that woman back from Kelly!" He struck the ground with a big fist. "We done wasted enough time already!"

"Lemme look at that wound," Ramsey said.

"It's all right, I tell you!"

"Lemme see it."

Concho's lips thinned; for an instant Ramsey thought he would refuse. But then the Negro sighed and lay down on his back.

Ramsey stripped away the crusted, filthy bandages carefully. The bullet-chopped flesh of Concho's side was a huge, scabby mess, with semiraw places showing through. Ramsey probed it carefully with his fingers. He could feel only a little fever around it, but that was normal, and no pockets of pus had formed.

"You see?" Concho said triumphantly. "It healin' fine. Not even any proud flesh."

Ramsey nodded and poured half the contents of the canteen into the hollow of a rock. As Concho watched, he began to rinse the dirty bandages as best he could. As soon as Concho realized what Ramsey was up to, he snapped: "I'll do that. You got no call to do that. It ain't yo' place to wash out my filth."

"Shut up," Ramsey said, "and lie still."

It took no time at all for the bandages to dry, and while they were far from clean when he put them back on Concho, they would keep a certain amount of dirt out of the wound and strap the shattered rib in place.

When it was done, Concho growled: "Much obliged."

"Por nada," Ramsey said. He got to his feet. "Keep a lookout. I'm goin' up th' mountain."

"What for?"

"What the hell you think for? You think I'm gonna let you lean on me all day? I'm gonna cut you a crutch off a piñon tree."

Concho grunted, but he made no protest.

When Ramsey returned, Concho got carefully to his feet and experimented with the crude crutch Ramsey had whittled. "This thing more trouble than it worth." He walked back and forth along the bench without it, erect, striding out. "See?"

"It won't be after you've gone five miles," Ramsey said. "Bring it along."

"Awright," Concho growled. "But you just like an old granny-woman."

He sat down, and now his restlessness was evident. "I been thinkin'," he said. "Here's the way I see it. By this time, your hawses are in good shape and Sheep's had time to git in touch with the Mescans. He'll have left Chilicotal Springs by now and gone on down to the Rio. By the time we git to Stewart's, he'll be layin' up at the old mine on Mariscal Mountain, and that's where we got to head from Stewart's. Your hawses will be gone by then, I reckon. The mine ain't far from the San Vicente crossin', and the Mescans will have already taken 'em across the river."

"I'm not worried about the horses," Ramsey said.

Concho looked at him strangely. His eyes glittered. Then he turned his head away without saying anything.

Between three and four, they clambered down to the spring, drank their fill, doused heads and faces, filled the canteen, and even the bladder of the pig, small as it was, which

74

Concho had taken out and cleaned and tied with a sinew from the hind leg. Then they set out across the badlands.

Which was what the country really was, for it was too mountainous, too cut with gulches, arroyos and canyons, too heaped with piles of loose gravel, like the tailings from some gigantic mine, for the word "desert" alone really to describe it. The heat was still brutal, of course, and it occurred to Ramsey that what they were really doing was making their way across the cinders of a huge furnace, as dwarfed by the huge and convulsed landscape as a couple of ants that had found their way into a grate full of glowing coals.

Concho led the way, moving with surprising speed at first —though he did not disdain to use the crutch. They kept, as far as possible, to cover, to the low ground, the bottoms of washes and draws and dry creek-beds with which the country was laced. It was not long before his own pace told on the Negro, and presently he slowed down. Ramsey was grateful, for the boots were rubbing his feet again, mercilessly. Concho's boots, flatter of heel, were better adapted for walking.

They camped that night at the bottom of an arroyo, rationing their water, ripping at the dried and leathery javelina flesh like wolves, shivering through the first few hours of darkness. When the slowly waxing moon rose and added its pale glimmer to starlight, they struck out again, through more nightmare terrain. By dawn, they had reached water at Neville Springs, and now the great bulk of the Chisos, its peaks soaring as much as four thousand feet up from the already elevated tableland, loomed over them. Concho became more furtive as the sun rose, for a watcher on the Chisos rim could spot them from miles away. Lame, exhausted, they slunk along through the comparative coolness of the early morning, until ten, when they found a covert in which to den up.

"We got to keep watch," Concho said now. "Kelly's men, Mescans, no tellin' who's liable to be along any minute. You git some rest; I keep an eye out."

Ramsey didn't argue; he was dead-beat. He had ridden horseback all his life and literally was capable of staying in the saddle for days, but he had never pretended to be a walker. In addition to the agony of his raw-rubbed feet, he was finding new muscles in his thighs and calves that he had never known he owned until now.

Besides, the long march seemed to have had a strange effect on Concho. Instead of exhausting him, it appeared to have built up his strength. For the last four hours, his speed had increased, although he still used the crutch, and though his side must have tortured him, his breathing was no longer stertorous and rasping, but deep and regular. It began to be apparent to Ramsey how really tough this man was. There was no self-concern in him; like an animal, given a while to lick his wounds, he was ready for any exertion again, completely free of the self-pity and self-protectiveness which would have kept any ordinary human immobile for days.

Ramsey got in two hours' drugged sleep; then Concho awakened him for his turn at watch. A couple of hours later, though the heat was at its worst, they moved on, keeping to whatever shade they could find. But desert noon was too much even for Concho; presently they stopped again, in a crease between two hills that were composed entirely of loose, piled gravel.

Late in the afternoon, they started out again. Far to the south, an immense escarpment reared itself, a wall of striated rock that glowed fantastically, gorgeously, in the final rays of the sun on the Mexican side of the river, Concho said, in Coahuila.

Now they fought their way through some of the worst country they had encountered yet. It was a nightmare of climbing in and out of defiles and up and down ridges. They stumbled over rocks and lost their footing in slides of loose gravel; their chaps deflected cactus thorns from their legs, but the brutal barbs of cholla that slid in with amazing ease lacerated their bodies above the waist. They circled and twisted and zigzagged, and Ramsey would have been completely lost if it had not been for the ever-present landmarks of the escarpment and the Chisos. But this detour, Concho said, was necessary. They had to avoid the traffic from the main crossings of the Rio at Boquillas and San Vicente, which moved up and down across the level land.

"We close to Chilicotal now," Concho told Ramsey when they rested before dawn. "That where they hold the stock when they bring it in. But if I right, they ain't nobody there now. We got to be careful, anyhow. We work our way around the foot of that there mountain yonder. It'll take us nigh on to all day, likely, but that's jest right, cause it'll bring us out to Stewart's ranch at nightfall. That's when we want to git there, in case somebody's camped around there."

Sam Ramsey, pulling the fishhook barbs of cholla from his arm, only grunted. Stewart's ranch, food, rest, weapons . . . these all seemed to him now only an impossible dream. They would never reach it. They were doomed to struggle across the desert forever, always tormented by hunger, thirst, and bleeding feet, clawed at by a thousand barbed plants, baked by sun and frozen by the night winds.

"Tomorrow night," Concho said. "Tomorrow night, man,

76

we'll eat . . ." He gnawed at the final remnant of javelina and tossed the last bone over his shoulder. Then he picked up his crutch and flung it from him, too. "Don't need that bastard no longer," he said. "It only slowin' me down, now." Then he arose. "Come on," he said. "We got some open country to cross, and we better git it done before daylight."

★ CHAPTER NINE ★

It was three hours after sundown the next night when they made Stewart's ranch—or what was left of it. The wooden outbuildings were only piles of ashes, their sun-dried timbers consumed completely by the flames. The ranch house itself, small, two-roomed, of adobe, had been gutted by fire as well; in the starlight, it was stark as a skull, its glassless windows like empty sockets, its tin roof collapsed inward. Only the corrals of pole and woven wire remained, their open gates creaking in the breeze. As his eyes swept the ruins, Sam Ramsey felt first a kind of sickness and then something of Concho's and Nora's anger. Here was a man's lifework destroyed, wantonly—waste, senseless waste.

"Denning and his outfit did a thorough job," Ramsey said thinly.

"Yeah, didn't they?" Concho grunted. He stood there motionless, arms at his sides, his big hands clenching and unclenching. Then he gave an odd, soft sigh. "Well, we still got them to deal with. Later."

The ruined ranch lay on a flat between two humped hills. Even its windmill had been burned, blades, gears, pipes, all a collapsed and twisted pile of metal in the ashes of the wooden tower. No water trickled now from the mouth of a pipe that fed two tanks, one for stock, the other carefully covered, for human consumption, and both tanks were dry. There was water, though, in a spring nearby, where the land fell away in a shelf. Cattle had trampled and muddied it. "The Mexes ain't rounded 'em all up yet," Concho grunted, as they drank.

"Where's the cave?" Ramsey asked.

Concho pointed to the east. "Up yonder on the mountainside. You can't see it from down here. I'm sure there ain't nobody found it yet. We always went up to it a different way each time, so's not to make any trail."

77

Ramsey's stomach growled with hunger. "Then let's go," he said.

Under cover of darkness, they crossed the flat, and then Ramsey followed Concho as the black man wove his way up a steep, talus-strewn slope, taking advantage of a network of small washes and gullies. They were at the cave before Ramsey even saw it: One moment, Concho was there; the next, he had vanished. When Ramsey blurted in surprise, Concho answered in a whisper: "In here." Then Ramsey saw the small crescent of darkness behind boulders on the narrow shelf they had reached. He dropped to hands and knees, wondering how many rattlers had taken refuge here tonight, and crawled in. He could see absolutely nothing, not even Concho, somewhere in there ahead of him.

Then a match flared. In its light, he saw that they were in a small, domed room of rock. Not much more than ten-by-twelve, its roof was just high enough for a man on his knees. The floor was clean-swept; along one wall were neatly stacked canned goods and rolled blankets. That much he glimpsed before the match went out. Concho muttered, struck another one, and then there was the more substantial light of a candle.

"See?" Concho said. "Ever'thing's still in order." He chuckled happily and slapped two cased rifles leaning against the blankets. "Even the guns and ammo! Me and Stewart put in many a hour's work here—see them water barrels along the back wall? We refilled 'em jest before Denning's outfit hit us." He scooped up some of the cans. "Beans and canned salmon, here—" And he tossed the food to Ramsey. "There a alcohol stove somewhere around here, but I ain't gonna wait to cook." He had found an opener and was already opening cans. When he was through, he tossed it to Ramsey and handed him a spoon.

They ate like wolves. And yet, surprisingly, their stomachs had shrunken so they could hold only a fraction of the contents of the cans. Then Concho began unrolling blankets. "Here you go, man. Us'll sleep tonight! Don't even hafta worry about keepin' any kinda guard."

Ramsey gingerly pulled off boots that seemed glued to his feet. His socks were a bloody pulp, his feet a stinking rawness. Concho, smoothing his own blanket pile, glanced up. Then he said, "Wait a minute, man. We got to take care of them feet."

"With what?" Ramsey said dryly, but Concho was already searching among the stores. When he turned around, he had a metal first-aid kit in his hand. He set it down, crawled to the back of the cave, and in a moment returned with a clean rag and a pan full of water in which there was a bar of soap. He sat down cross-legged at the end of Ramsey's blankets. "Lemme have the right one first."

"You can't—" Ramsey protested, but Concho already had his ankle. "You washed out them bandages of mine, didn't you?" he grunted. Then, as gently as any woman could have, he sponged the dirt away from raw flesh. Ramsey bit his lip as iodine stung him. After which, adeptly, Concho applied bandages of gauze and tape. Then he crawled to the entrance with the pan of water and dumped it.

When he came back, Ramsey said, "Much obliged."

"Por nada," Concho said, not looking at Ramsey. "I wish to hell we had some boots and socks up here. Them rider's boots ain't worth a damn for what we got to do. But maybe the tape'll make it easier." He crawled into his blankets and pulled them up about him. "Good night," he said, and in a moment his snore filled the cave.

Ramsey slid down in the blankets. For the first time in days, his feet were free of pain; now there was only a throbbing ache that, by contrast, was almost pleasurable. As the blankets trapped his body's warmth, he slid easily into his first good sleep in a week.

What awakened him was a sound; and it brought him upright out of unconsciousness—though he could not place it, an alarm of some sort. Then he heard it again, and in the pie-slice of sunlight that fell through the cave entrance, he saw Concho working a rifle bolt, the weapon across his knees, an open box of ammunition beside him.

Before he could speak, Concho said: "Easy. We got company." He pointed to the mouth of the cave; then, with the gun cradled in his arm, he crawled forward, out onto the boulder-rimmed shelf beyond the cave's entrance.

Blinking sleep away, Ramsey seized the other weapon, pulled it from its case, and scooped up a clip of cartridges. With his heart pounding, but the weight of the '03 Springfield good and reassuring against him, he crawled after Concho. They had slept late. Outside, the sun was hot and bright.

Concho lay on his belly, peering through a natural rifle port between two rocks. Ramsey squirmed up beside him and Concho moved to let him look. Squinting against the light, Ramsey saw, spread out on the flat nearly a half mile below them the ruins of the ranch. Then he drew in his breath. Two saddled horses were tethered to the wire of the corral. And two men—they wore the high-crowned *charro* hats and tight pants of Mexicans—were poking at the ashes of a burned out-building.

79

"Who are they?" Ramsey whispered, though it would be impossible for normal speech to be heard at that distance.

There was a strange grin on Concho's face. "Unlucky folks," the Negro said in a natural voice. "A couple of *Revolucionarios* passin' through. They jest had to stop and poke around to see if there's anything left they could steal."

"They alone?"

"Yeah," Concho said. "That's how come they unlucky." Then Ramsey saw that he had passed his arm through the sling of the rifle and drawn it tight.

"Wait!" Ramsey heard himself blurt. "What are you gonna do?"

Concho was up on his knees, now, an elbow braced on top of a rock. He pushed the stock of the rifle into his shoulder tightly. "Git us some hawses," he said.

"But you can't just—" Ramsey bit off the words. Cold-blooded murder, he thought, staring at the unsuspecting men. One of them was squatting as he poked into the ashes; the other walked in circles around the building's ruins. "You can't possibly hit 'em at this distance," Ramsey finished. "All you'll do is warn 'em we're here."

Concho did not answer. He was squinting down the rifle barrel. Then he raised his head, adjusted the field sight. "That oughta be about right," he murmured, not to Ramsey, but to himself. "And there ain't a bit of wind."

"Concho—" Ramsey began again; and then he shut up and began to load his own rifle. Concho was a natural force, raw, unstoppable—like a rockslide or a flash flood. And these men, if Concho's arm was good, were doomed. But if Concho missed, Ramsey would have to try to kill them, too. Once warned, they could not be allowed to escape.

Though they were nearly a half mile distant, the morning air was so clear that Ramsey could see them in detail. The one who had been squatting got to his feet and gestured to his companion with the stick he had used to stir the ashes. The sun glinted off gold braid in the brim of his sombrero and off the huge rowels of the spurs on his black leather boots. The other, taller, but not so richly dressed, nodded, as if receiving an order. Then he turned and walked toward the horses and the rifle thundered in Ramsey's ears as Concho shot him in the back. He pitched forward on his face, heavily, and lay still.

The other man stared, frozen, transfixed. Then he whirled, head swiveling wildly, and Ramsey would have sworn he could see the whites of his eyes. Suddenly he began to run toward the horses, and Concho fired again.

He missed. A puff of dust bloomed at the heels of the running man.

Ramsey heard Concho's growled curse, the snick of the bolt, and the third shot, all blurred together in a single sound.

The runner tripped, fell to his knees. He tried to rise; Concho fired again, and he collapsed.

Concho turned to Ramsey, his big lips twisted in a triumphant grin. "There you are," he said.

"Yeah," said Ramsey. "There we are."

Concho ejected the spent round, locked another in the chamber. "Now, we jest lay doggo for a spell to make sure that shooting don't bring nobody else." He put his eye to the aperture between the rocks. "I'll keep watch out here. Why don't you open us up some breakfast?"

Vultures were already wheeling high overhead when Concho at last deemed it safe to go down and claim the horses. With food packed into blanket rolls and their filled canteens from the cave slung over their shoulders, Ramsey and the Negro skittered down the slope and warily crossed the flat, guns ready. But they made the ruins of the ranch without alarm, and Concho went first to the man who had run and turned him over with his boot. Dark, sightless eyes stared skyward from a flat-nosed face with high cheekbones and a gash of a mouth.

"Yaqui Injun," Concho said. "That means he likely from Leon Sanchez' outfit. Sanchez has got a lot of Yaquis in his bunch. That's good; I'm glad they Sanchez' men and not Villa's."

"I thought Sanchez was part of Villa's army."

"Everybody in the North part of Villa's army now," Concho said. "That because he winnin'. But Sanchez waited a long time before he took sides. Long enough so Pancho ain't goin' to trouble himself about two of Sanchez' men bein' bushwhacked. If they was his own, soon as he found out about it, he wouldn't rest 'til he'd hunted us down like wolves."

"Just the same," Ramsey said, "it might not be a bad idea to haul these bodies off and bury 'em."

"That just what I was thinkin'," Concho said. Then he squatted and began tugging at the dead man's boots. "These too good to throw away. They got flatter heels and look like they oughta fit you."

"I don't want 'em," Ramsey said.

Concho didn't even look up. "Don't be a damn fool," he said.

Even without socks, the boots were very comfortable. The

81

bodies yielded, as well, two six-guns and plenty of ammunition for each. In saddle scabbards were Winchester rifles, and there was a bandolier of ammunition across each saddle pommel. The horses were good, but skittish, flanks marked by the big spurs, mouths ruined by spade bits. That discovery caused the last tatters of Ramsey's regret at the ambush to vanish. The saddles were Mexican, with enormous flat horns and smooth-worn wooden seats.

They loaded the dead men across the saddles and led the horses for nearly two miles. At last, at the foot of a big hill that was only a mound of sand, gravel, and shale, its only growth a few clumps of cactus, Concho halted. "Here," he said. They unloaded the bodies and laid them in a hollow at the foot of the hill. Then, as agile as a jaguar, Concho ran up the side of the mound. Halfway up, he circled around until he was above the corpses and began to stamp his huge feet, pushing down rocks and gravel, digging out sand. Suddenly he jumped aside as a full-sized slide developed, boiling down the hillside in a cloud of dust. Tumbling rocks and gravel poured down in a cascade; when the high swirl of dust had settled, the bodies were entombed.

Concho half ran, half slid back down. "The wind blow out what tracks we left," he said. "A day's time and nobody ever know what happened to 'em." He took the reins of his horse from Ramsey and swung up into the saddle, his eyes gleaming. "Plenty of guns and two good hawses. We don't git Nora back now, it our own damn fault. Come on, less ride. We kin make Sheep Kelly's hide-out at the Mariscal mine by sunset, easy!"

It was good to be armed and on horseback again. Ramsey felt renewed and invigorated. Sheep Kelly might have twenty men, Concho had said, and they would all be experienced fighters. Nevertheless, Ramsey no longer felt that the odds were impossible. He had no idea what lay ahead of them, but whatever it was, he felt equal to it once again—especially with Concho at his side.

As Concho led him by a devious route, always keeping to cover, it dawned on Ramsey that the big Negro was the first really professional fighting man he'd ever seen in action; and that they were a breed apart. Sam Ramsey himself had been too young to sign up when the recruiter for the Rough Riders had passed through North Wells. And even as he was growing up, the old days of West Texas had passed: The Apaches were subdued; the Texas and Southwestern Cattle Raiser's Association had rustling well in hand; the government of Mexico seemed stable, and the border had been quiet. Until that night in his horse pasture, he personally had never been the target of a shot fired in anger, nor had he fired one himself.

Now, he thought, he had changed. Somewhere along the way, the old Sam Ramsey had been lost and a new one had taken over. The man who called himself Ramsey now was like a tool tempered in fire and then annealed to new hardness. The new Ramsey looked at the old one and found him pathetic. The Sam Ramsey who had started out alone in blissful ignorance of the country he was entering and the kind of men he was going up against wouldn't have lasted for the flicker of a match flame. But the new Sam Ramsey—the man he was now—was equal to whatever came. He had learned the virtues of endurance and caution and especially ruthlessness. And he had also learned that it was better not to be alone.

That, he thought, watching Concho's broad back rise and fall ahead of him, was the biggest change. Always, he had treasured his aloneness, his self-sufficiency. Now, it no longer seemed anything to treasure. Nor did he feel alone any more. Not only was there Concho, riding ahead of him, ready to fight alongside him, but there was Nora Stewart, too. Somehow she had entered his life, in the few short hours he had known her, and had become important to him—more important than his horses, more important than his aloneness, more important than his very life. It was strange, he thought, and nothing he could now make head or tail out of . . . but he was no longer a man alone.

The sun rose to zenith, blazed down on them, baked them in a way to which he had now become accustomed; and as it finally slid down the brazen sky, Concho gestured toward the hump of a huge mountain not far distant to the south. "Yonder's Mariscal," he said. "That's where the old mercury mine was. And that's where Sheep Kelly hangs out now, and that's where he'll have Miz Stewart."

Ramsey tilted back his hat. The mountain ran almost north-south, its crest a good fifteen hundred feet above the flatlands. Like all mountains in this geological hell, its flanks seemed almost naked, devoid of cover.

Concho was swinging down off his horse. "We'll shelter up here in this arroyo 'til dark. Then we'll go size up the lay of the land."

Ramsey dismounted behind the cover of a high cutbank and loosened his horse's cinches. When he turned around, Concho was squatting, drawing a kind of map in the sand with a branch of ocotillo.

"Look here," Concho said. He traced a triangle that had to

83

be the mountain. "The front of it points out towards the desert. The back of it here drops off into a canyon, down to the Rio. Now, out here on the flats, around the front, there's about a dozen 'dobe huts, where the mine workers used to live. Most of 'em are spaced pretty far apart. Right in the middle of 'em, there's the mine super's house. It's twicet as big as the others and made outa wood and concrete. My guess is that Sheep Kelly'll have tooken it over for hisself, and Nora—if he ain't already tired of her—will be in there with 'im."

Ramsey nodded.

"Now," Concho said, "they don't hafta worry about the back of the mountain. Nobody can git at 'em from the Rio side. But out here in front, on the desert, Sheep'll have a perimeter guard." He drew a half circle that encompassed the flanks of the mountain and the dots he'd made to indicate the cluster of houses.

"Where's the mine itself?" Ramsey asked.

Concho's pointer moved up the triangle a fourth of the distance from the apex. "Right here. There's some shafts and some old buildin's. If anybody was to attack Sheep and his men, they could retreat back up here to the mine and hold off a whole army. If they got pushed, they could go back over the mountain to the canyon, git down somehow—there's bound to be a trail—and cross the Rio."

"Looks like a tough place to crack," Ramsey said.

"Tough enough," Concho said. He tapped the end of the stick where he had drawn the mine. "There's a ridge runs up here, above the mine. They'll have a guard on it, too. From there, a man can overlook the whole damn country."

He tossed the stick aside, and the two men sat down on opposite sides of the map. Ramsey stared at it for a while. Then he said, "We got to come up the back side of the mountain and take that guard on the ridge."

Concho nodded and smiled, as pleased as a teacher hearing a recitation by a star pupil. "Now you got it," he said. "That's where we git the lay of the land." He took out a pack of Mexican cigarettes found on one of the bodies, and rammed one in his mouth. He snapped a match and looked at Ramsey across the flame. "There's jest one thing to remember," he said. "It's gonna be you and me against twenty men, and the first one that lets the other down, he's signin' both our death warrants. Now, somebody got to be in charge of an operation like this. Let's git this settled now. Who it gonna be, you or me?"

Ramsey looked at him a moment. Then he said, "I reckon it'll be you. This is more in your line."

Concho looked faintly surprised, and he was not smiling now. "I jest wanted to have it understood. I mean, you a white man and . . . and I black. If—"

Ramsey said quietly, "I'd just about forgot that until you reminded me." Then he spat into the dust. "You're the expert. Call the turn and I'll follow orders."

They stayed hidden in the arroyo for a long time—too long, it seemed to Ramsey. He watched the setting sun paint the flanks of Mariscal Mountain bright red, saw it strike gleams from the Chisos, not far to the north. Then darkness settled, and in the distance, watching from the rim of the arroyo, they saw pinpoints of light around the foot of the mountain. Concho drew in a deep, satisfied breath. "They're there," he whispered.

They ate cold beans and salmon again, and the sliver of moon arose over the escarpment and mountains to the southeast. Its glow, mingled with starlight, silvered the flats before them, transforming the harsh rawness of the desert to a blue fantasy, laced with shadows of darker blue. Still Concho did not move, and Ramsey's pocket watch told him it was getting close to midnight.

At last Concho arose. "We kin start now. Wanted to wait to hit 'em jest about two in the morning. A man's at his lowest, you wake him outa sleep about then. Even if he's on guard, he ain't alert. Come on. We ride a ways, then we walk a ways."

They mounted up, and Concho led the way down the draw. Presently they climbed out to level ground. Ahead, the mountain was like some huge animal sleeping in the darkness. The pinpoints of light had vanished now, all but one or two.

"What they got to worry about?" Concho said as they rode across a shadowed flat. "They figger I'm dead and prob'ly you, too. They know them people from North Wells have had all they want. Maybe the Army'll come in—but no troop of cavalry's gonna sneak up on anybody. And Rangers—? They all chasin' that other cow-thief, Chico Cana, over around Presidio. Still, Sheep keeps good discipline, army discipline. He'd shoot a man he found asleep on guard." He made a clucking sound in his throat. "In a way, you got to admire a man like Sheep, runs his outfit the way he does. I know Villa's made him several offers to hire out with him but Sheep thinks it's safer and more money jest to lift cattle and sell to the armies."

He quit talking then, for they were swinging a wide circle that brought them to broken ground. An hour later, when they had come out of it, they were in the very shadow of the mountain itself. Now, only one light gleamed on the flat in front of the mountain's toe. Concho reined in and swung down, pointing at it. His mouth close to Ramsey's ear, he whispered: "I bet that Sheep hisself up this late. I don't even wanta think why." Then the rasp of hatred ebbed from his tone. "We tie the hawses here and go on foot. When we climb outa this draw, take a good look around and memorize the landmarks, so you can git here in a hurry if they after you."

They took the Springfields from their saddles and slung them over their shoulders. The horses they tethered to clumps of brush. Then Concho led the way up out of the draw in which they'd halted. As they gained the level ground, Concho paused. Ramsey saw that he had drawn a knife taken from one of the Mexicans, was testing its edge with his thumb.

Keeping their way to whatever cover they found, they worked their way toward the mountain. Ahead of Ramsey, Concho was a wraith, a soundless shadow floating across the desert, from this boulder to that yucca, scouting, then beckoning Ramsey on.

Sam Ramsey himself moved almost without sound. He had hunted enough to know how to travel quietly, testing each step before putting weight on his foot, careful not to hurry if hurrying would cause him to make any noise.

Presently they reached the foot of the mountain. It rose, a jumbled pile of rock and cactus, abruptly from the desert floor. Its flank was a steep patchwork of shadows and starlight. Concho edged through the rolling ground along its foot a distance, headed toward the base of the triangle, toward the Rio. Then, abruptly, he stopped short and in a smooth, melting motion, dropped flat, disappearing in shadow. Five yards behind him, Ramsey immediately and instinctively followed suit before he saw the cause of alarm.

Down like this, he could see it better, anyhow. From this angle, the head and shoulders of the man standing beside a shoulder-high outthrust of ground from the mountain was silhouetted against the sky. The guard had his back against the side of the hill; a cigarette glowed in his mouth; a rifle was cradled in his arm. He was looking away from them, toward the east.

Silently, Ramsey drew his pistol, but Concho was already wriggling forward on his belly, propelling himself with elbows and knees. Like an enormous snake, he began to cover the twenty yards that separated them from the guard, and his progress was fantastically without sound.

Now Concho had vanished in the darkness. The guard

86

straightened up, and the cigarette made a winking arc as he tossed it through the air. Ramsey saw the little shower of sparks it made when it hit the ground. The guard cleared his throat and shifted the rifle to his other arm. Minutes passed, and Ramsey lay motionless, but with his Colt ready. Hardly daring to breathe, he wondered what had become of the Negro.

Sudenly there was sound, a thump and crashing of brush. It came from a dozen yards in front of the guard, towards the east. Instantly, the man was alert. He straightened up, took three long steps forward, raising his rifle. "Who's there?" he snapped in a harsh voice. *"Quien es?"*

Then, like a ghost materializing, a black shape reared up behind him. Ramsey caught the silhouette of a raised knife; then the blackness blotted the guard from his vision. There was a curious muffled sound, a thick gurgle, and the blackness that was Concho lowered the body, turned, and beckoned Ramsey to come forward to where the man lay in a welter of blood from a cut throat. The body was still moving slightly when Ramsey stepped across it.

Concho's teeth flashed white in darkness. "That's one down. Now, we go up the mountain."

Its dark wall loomed above them, rearing almost a quarter-mile high. Concho led Ramsey through a nest of boulders and struck a trail of sorts—a trail made for goats, Ramsey thought, as he panted after the Negro. Winding, twisting, it led almost straight up, and Ramsey groped blindly after Concho's silent presence. The slung rifle banged against his back; sometimes it would clack against a rock, or a piece of shale, dislodged by hand or foot would go rattling down. Then they would freeze, on whatever precarious perch they found themselves, holding breaths until they were sure the way was clear.

All at once, the trail gave out entirely. Ahead of them was a black vee, a split in a wall of rock. Concho unslung his rifle, pressed it to his chest, and then moved sideways into that cleft. It was so narrow that Ramsey, following him, had to suck in his belly. But it led upward, and their feet made no sound on its floor of drifted sand. It was also, Ramsey thought sourly, a perfect trap if they were discovered. From above, they could be slain like fish in a barrel.

They were in it for fifteen minutes. Then a vee of sky showed at one end, only to be blotted by Concho's body. In a moment, they emerged from the cleft onto a narrow bench. Now, above them, the mountain rounded off. Concho let Ramsey breathe a moment, and, as if feeling the effects of the wound, himself seemed grateful for the rest.

Then they climbed again. This time, Concho led the way with drawn revolver, hunkered down behind the skyline. Ramsey followed, bent low in the same way. Ahead of them, he could see the long, razor-edged crest of this ridge of the mountain, black against the star-powdered sky.

They reached it, on hands and knees now, and then Concho sank flat on his belly. Ramsey dropped beside him.

In front of them, the ridge dipped down to a shallow, sandy hollow. Then the mountain rose again, to another crest perhaps twenty feet higher than the one on which they lay.

Ramsey and Concho scanned it. Then Ramsey tensed, tapped Concho on the arm. The Negro followed Ramsey's pointing hand and nodded. Boulders, silhouetted, strewed the other ridge crest, and among a clump of them directly at their front, the head and shoulders of a man wearing a flat-brimmed, peak-crowned army hat was almost lost in the jumble of shapes.

Silently, Concho holstered his Colt and once more drew his knife. He thrust its blade significantly under Ramsey's nose. Ramsey understood and shoved his own revolver back into the leather. Then he pulled his sheath knife.

Soundless as fog, Concho moved over the ridge crest. He seemed to swim across the ground, like a fish in water. Ramsey, less adept, followed slowly and awkwardly, taking no chances on giving the alarm. Within a dozen feet, his palms were full of cactus thorns, some had even pierced the leather of his chaps, and Concho had left him far behind.

Now Concho was working his way up the back slope of the ridge ahead. The man sat among the boulders unawares, the end of his cigarette an occasional bright wink as he smoked. Ramsey reached the sandy trough between ridges and halted there to get his breath. But Concho was almost to the top of the other ridge.

Then the Negro reared to his feet, a huge shape against the sky. In a strange, great, shambling leap, he covered the rest of the distance. Ramsey saw it all in silhouette, the man alarmed, rising, turning, the big hand reaching out to cup his face, the rise and fall of the knife . . .

Then, without warning, almost at Concho's back, another figure reared itself. "What the hell?" it blurted, and Ramsey saw a pistol coming up, even as Concho struck again with the knife, unaware of this menace behind him.

Sam Ramsey sprang to his feet. He never knew how he made it up that slope in such close-shaved seconds. But the man with the gun heard him coming, and that was what saved Concho's life. The guard froze, confused, jerked his head around, and then, in a flying leap, Ramsey was on him.

There was the white blur of the face beneath the straw skimmer, the dark hole of a mouth opening to yell. Ramsey literally thrust his hand straight into that, even as he struck with the knife, low and awkwardly, driving the blade deep, ripping upward.

There was no scream. Teeth closed on his hand and he forced the head backward with a savage jerk. Then the knife grated horribly on a rib, deflected, Ramsey pulled it out and struck again, this time for the heart. The man fell backwards, gun spilling from his hand, and Ramsey was on top of him, hand still plugging the gagging mouth, using the knife like a butcher, wherever he could find a target, until the body beneath him was limp and still. Then Ramsey rolled away, bile hot in his mouth, his left hand bleeding, his shirtfront drenched with blood, and looked up to see Concho crouching over him.

"Man," Concho whispered, "you sho' did go for his chit-'lins. I'm a goddam fool, never thought there'd be two . . ."

Ramsey did not answer. If he unclenched his teeth, he was certain to vomit. He got to his knees, hating the red wetness of the cloth that brushed his belly. Then he swallowed hard, and, miraculously, he was all right except for a shaking in the legs.

"If I'd seen this thing first," Concho muttered, "I'da known. Generally, it better with two men to work one." He plucked at Ramsey's sleeve. "Come, look what them jokers had over here." There was a strange exultancy in his voice.

Ramsey crawled toward the nest of boulders, avoiding the body of the man whose throat Concho had cut. The Negro crouched over a weapon of some sort that was mounted on a low bipod, its barrel pointing down the mountain. "What is it?" Ramsey asked.

Concho almost giggled with happiness as he dropped down behind it. "Man, don't you know what this is? This a Lewis gun. Ole Sheep Kelly playin' in the big time now—he done gone and got himself one of the best machine guns they make!"

★ CHAPTER TEN ★

The gun had been set up to command the forward slope of the mountain and the tableland beneath it. Ramsey, squatting beside Concho in the boulders looked over the edge of the gun position. Under its muzzle, the ridge sloped sharply, until it reached a small bench on which were two stone buildings almost like towers and a cluster of smaller sheds.

That was the old mercury mine. Below it, the mountain continued downward, split by a deep draw half-clogged with cinnabar tailings. On either side of the draw, the mountain was divided into jutting, sloping wings, and a scratch of a road ran down the rocky top of each wing to the level land a half mile below. Out on the flat, there was the widely scattered handful of huts and shacks, all dark except for a single light that burned in a larger structure in the middle.

Concho swung the gun as happily as a child with a toy, traversing, elevating, depressing, two extra ammunition drums in his lap. Ramsey drew back and asked, "You know how to work this thing?"

"Man, what you think I did with Pancho Villa? I was his instructor. Hell, I can play a tune on this booger. Kelly musta traded Pancho outa this for some hawses or cows."

"Then that settles it," Ramsey said.

"Settles what?"

Ramsey picked up the straw skimmer the man he had killed had worn. Lyman had worn a straw hat—but Ramsey did not look at the corpse's face. "That it's me who goes down yonder after Nora," he said and settled the hat on his head.

"Now, wait a minute—," Concho whispered.

"Listen, dammit. You're the one knows how to work this machine gun. I'll need you up here to cover me. Besides, I can pass for one of Kelly's men in the dark, but they'd recognize you in a minute. Was that *hombre* wearin' chaps?"

Concho groped. "No."

"Then I'll take mine off." Ramsey unbuckled them.

"Listen," Concho said, "how you aim to work it?"

"I don't see but one way." Ramsey laid the chaps aside. "That big house used to belong to the superintendent, didn't it? Well, won't Kelly be in it now?"

"I guess so," Concho said.

"Then that's where Nora'll be. I've got to go down there, size up the situation when I git there, and take Nora out the best way I can."

Concho was silent for a moment. Then he said, "Suppose Kelly ain't alone? And even if he is, there ain't nobody any worse in a fight than him. 'Fore he deserted the Army, he was in Cuba and the Philippines both. He got medals, man. Goin' up against him ain't no job for a amateur."

"I can handle it," Ramsey said.

90

Even in the dark he was aware of Concho's scrutiny. The big Negro's eyes seemed to bore into him like augers. Then Concho said quietly, "Yeah, I reckon you can."

He slapped the machine gun lightly. "Okay. You go down, and I'll cover you from up here. Git Nora and head straight for the hawses. If it's a clean gitaway, I'll meet you there. But if there's shootin', don't worry about me. You reach them critters, you mount up and hightail it. Me and the Lewis gun will discourage any son that takes a notion to follow you."

"Hell, we can't do that. You'd be afoot."

"Goddammit," Concho said, "I was afoot when I met up with you. Now you do what I say." Ramsey could see his eyes in the dark. "We agreed who's givin' the orders here, remember?"

Ramsey hesitated, then nodded. "All right. But try to make it to the horses if you can." He stepped over the edge, beside the gun, and began to work his way downward.

From the darkness above, Concho's voice was a hiss. "Good luck . . ."

Sam Ramsey did not reply. He had all he could do to watch his footing. There had to be a path somewhere for them to have got this gun up, but he couldn't find it. Despite all his caution, rocks rolled as he made his way down, and their bouncing and clatter seemed like thunder. After each slide, he halted, freezing, half expecting challenge or gunfire. But there was no alarm, and he went on and, after what seemed centuries, reached the sheltering flank of one of the stone towers.

Here he halted and took a closer look at what lay below. The road on his left would bring him down to the flat and among the buildings most directly, but at the bottom of the mountain it would take him within three yards of the door of an adobe hut with a pole corral behind it, in which Ramsey could see the shifting dark shapes of at least two-dozen horses.

But the shack was dark and he would pass the corral at enough distance not to spook the horses with his strangeness or the scent of fresh blood on his shirt. He thought of Nora, down there with a man Concho had described as mad, and he took the shortest way.

Cautiously, he moved out of the shadows onto the road. It lay full in the sheen of starlight and the sickle moon, and now he straightened up and struck out at a normal gait, as if he belonged here and had business down below. But he never took his hand from his gun butt, and he felt sickeningly naked and exposed, though reason told him that it was unlikely there were more guards within that outer cordon.

Striding along openly like that, he made good speed. Below, that one light still burned in the old superintendent's house, mocking him, challenging him. What was going on in there? His mind conjured pictures that made his stomach roil, and it took all his self-control to keep from breaking into a run.

Later, he would remember that journey as one of the longest in his life. On and on he went, every sense, every nerve, alert; and now a new worry nagged at him. Suppose Nora wasn't in that lighted house? Suppose Sheep Kelly had chosen another house for his own . . . or suppose he had already tired of Nora and passed her along? Suppose—

He halted. He was almost off the mountain now, and in a moment, he would have to pass the hut that sat beside the trail. His eyes searched it for any sign of life, but if it had occupants, they were sleeping. Not far behind it, horses stamped and shifted in the corral. He stared at that, too, but could see no guard over the animals. At last he went ahead, fighting the urge to crouch and sneak.

He came up to the hut, passed it without incident, and was a few feet beyond it when several horses whinnied in the corral and there was the thud of hoofbeats. Ramsey froze, first appalled by the bugle-call loudness of that neighing, and then, as it rang again, tingling with recognition. In the pale starlight, he saw nearly a half-dozen animals crowding up to the fence, and there was loud nickering, snorting.

For an instant, then, Nora was forgotten, Sheep Kelly, Concho, everything but the horses. His Morgans—Gibson Girl, Sunrise, all the rest of his best geldings, and now more crowding up behind them. Ramsey took a step toward the corral, then halted.

There was no time. He turned away, full of bitterness. So Kelly had not sold all the herd, had kept the best for himself. He had come so far, endured so much, to find those animals only a few yards away, and now they might as well be on the moon . . .

Then a voice rang out from the adobe hut. "Whut the hell's wrong with them hawses?" Ramsey saw the white blur of a face in the dark square of a glassless window. "Who's out there?"

Ramsey cleared his throat. "It's me," he said in the most toneless voice he could muster. "Reckon I spooked 'em."

There was a moment's silence. Then: "It's only Lyman; I can see that damfool hat. What's the matter, Lyman, something wrong up yonder?"

"No. Ran outa tobacco." Then Ramsey turned away and strode on, praying that Lyman was not an occupant of that hut, did not keep his makings there. His back almost ached with its vulnerability, and he was ready to jump and run at the first sign of alarm.

But none came. Only a mutter from the hut. "Goddam hawses. A man can't git no sleep near this corral." Ramsey hurried on, his heart pounding, his ears closed to the sound of nickering behind him.

So it had been Lyman, he thought. That much score evened, anyhow.

★ ★ ★

Now he was on level ground, fully inside the little settlement of adobe houses. The miners' huts had been scattered all over the flat like blocks thrown down at random, but all of them were a respectful distance from the big house with the front porch and tin roof, where the light burned. And now that was only fifty yards away.

Ramsey halted, trying to decide his next move. From here on, he would have to move silently. Even if Kelly took him for a guard, he would come out to question him if he heard him.

There was no cover between himself and the light that spilled out that back window, except the rickety shape of an ancient, awry privy not far from the rear of the house. In a moment, Ramsey left the trail and circled to come up beside that, to gain the cover of the pool of shadow it cast. He moved soundlessly; it was easy on the deep sand that now cushioned his tread.

He reached the side of the privy and flattened himself against the structure's wall. Now, for the first time, he drew his gun. From here, he could look into the lighted window, but all he could see was a section of wall and door.

Then a figure moved into the square of light and paused. Ramsey saw plainly a skinny, narrow-shouldered torso in a dirty undershirt. Above it was a strange face of almost surpassing ugliness—wooly, iron-gray hair, a huge, rounded nose that curved down almost over the mouth, and virtually no chin at all. Ramsey could even see the nervous twitch of the upper lip and the nostrils, a constant flicker that revealed stained teeth. There was no doubt any longer as to who occupied this house or how he had got his name.

Then, almost as if Sheep Kelly were possessed of some sixth sense—or maybe he'd caught the disturbance at the corral—he strode to the open window and looked out. In one hand, he held a glass, in the other, a bottle. With them poised, he stared into the night, and ludicrous as his other features were, the eyes that seemed to look directly at Ramsey were no laughing matter. Like bits of onyx or obsidian, they swept the darkness; then, after an endless thirty seconds, Kelly turned away. Now his back was a perfect target, but one Ramsey could not afford to shoot at. Ramsey held his breath, listening.

Through the window came the murmur of voices. One of them was masculine, but nevertheless thin and high, like the rasp of a saw in hardwood. The other was only a toneless whisper which Ramsey could not identify. But now he knew that Kelly was not alone.

It must be Nora in there with him! Ramsey thought, and his pulse quickened. Simultaneously, all nervousness left him; now he was so cool and controlled and ready for anything that he himself was astonished.

Kelly's torso moved out of the light; when it was gone, Ramsey, his decision made, left the shadows. He eared back the hammer of the gun gently, to make only the tiniest click. Then he padded cautiously around to the front of the house.

It was dark, a porch running its full width. Ramsey stepped up, groped his way until he found a door. He turned the knob and applied gentle pressure.

The latch slipped out; the door swung inward perhaps a quarter of an inch, then was blocked. Kelly had bolted it. Ramsey cursed silently. Then he clenched his fist and hammered loudly, urgently, on the door.

Inside the house, another door opened and dim light fell into the front room. That buzz-saw voice called out tensely, "Who the hell is that?"

Ramsey let his shoulders and his head with the straw skimmer appear briefly in the window beside the door; he knew Kelly could see him only in silhouette. "It's Lyman," he called loudly. "There's trouble."

A curse answered him as he pulled away from the window. Then there was the quick pad of feet. Ramsey stepped back from the door. He heard the bolt slide; the door swung open. Kelly's long underwear made him a white blur in the darkness. "Lyman?" he snapped, and there was suspicion in his voice and he held a gun outthrust. Ramsey had drawn his knife and now he stepped forward, inside the gun, and rammed both the knife and pistol against the man's belly.

"Drop it," he said. He pushed hard with the knife.

Kelly's body went rigid. Ramsey heard his indrawn breath. Then Kelly's gun thudded on the floor of the porch.

"Inside," Ramsey said, forcing the man backwards.

They were face to face. Kelly's breath was foul, laden with the anise scent of mescal. Kelly said, as Ramsey pushed the door shut with his heel, "What the hell?"

"First wrong move, I kill you," Ramsey said. "Where is she?"

Kelly was silent for a couple of seconds. Then he said, "The woman? You come after her?"

"That's right."

"She's in the other room." There was a strange undertone in Kelly's voice; Ramsey did not think it was entirely fear.

"Alone?"

Why, it was almost amusement. "Alone," Kelly said.

"All right," Ramsey said. He pushed the man backwards toward the other room. Kelly moved with docility. Ramsey didn't like that, either. Kelly's shoulders pushed the door fully open, and Ramsey followed him into the room.

It was small, and even with the window up, it stank—whiskey, mescal, Mexican tobacco, and unwashed bodies. There was a table in a corner, clothes thrown across it, a bed against the wall, piled high with rumpled blankets all in a tangle.

"Nora!" Ramsey rapped.

"She's drunk, buddy," Sheep Kelly said. His nose and mouth were twitching rapidly, but his eyes were steady. "Out like a light." He jerked his head toward the bed, and that was when Ramsey saw her leg and foot protruding from the pile of blankets.

"For Christ's sake," Ramsey said, full of dismay. This was the one thing he had not counted on. Then he said, "You're lyin'."

A strange, ropy chuckle seemed to come from Kelly's chest. "All right," he said. "See for yourself."

Ramsey stuck the knife in his belt. Keeping the gun trained on Kelly, he moved sideways to the bed and seized the leg. He pulled it hard. "Nora!" he snapped. "Wake up."

The leg did not even move.

Still without taking his eyes off Kelly, who stood there with hands meekly half-raised, Ramsey seized the covers and yanked them away. Nora lay sprawled, face-down, her hair a tangle. Ramsey slapped her hard. "Goddammit, Nora, wake up!"

Her body only shifted slightly, and she made a sick sound in her throat.

"All right," Kelly said. "She's all yours, friend. If you want her, you can have her. All you got to do is git her out." In the midst of its twitching, the loose-lipped mouth did something that might have been a grin. "I want to see how you do it."

"You won't be alive to," Ramsey said, with exactly as much ferocity as he felt.

"Then neither will you," Kelly said. "You think you can carry a dead-drunk woman past my guards? They'll kill you both." The lamplight glinted on a small metal chain around his neck as he jerked his head at Nora. "She's been drunk fer two days."

Ramsey's eyes never left Kelly, as he groped, found Nora's arm, and pulled her roughly onto her back. He heard the hoarse rasp of her breathing. He slapped her face. "Nora! Nora, it's Sam Ramsey."

Finally she spoke. "For God's sake, Sheep," she mumbled. "Don't hit me any more."

That was when Ramsey let his eyes shuttle away from the outlaw, and what he saw made him draw in breath. Her right eye was a huge, swollen, purple mass, the blue-green bruise ran all the way down the right cheek. Her bottom lip was cut and puffy. And her body piebald with more bruises.

"She took some taming," Kelly said casually. "She'd done forgot how it was."

Ramsey said, "I'm going to kill you now."

Kelly said, "You do, and you die too. Look, friend, I've had her all I want. You're welcome to her. I'll make you a deal. You don't kill me, I'll give you safe conduct outa here with her. Hell, I'll have my men carry her to your horses for you, and if you ain't got none, I'll give you some."

Ramsey didn't answer him. He got Nora's wrist and pulled. "Nora," he said pleadingly, urgently. "Nora, you got to wake up. It's Sam Ramsey . . ."

"Dead," she mumbled. But she was sitting up now. She buried her face in her hands. "Dead. Concho, too."

"I'm not. It's Ramsey. I'm alive. I've come for you."

She raised her head; Ramsey had shifted to where he could see her and Kelly at the same time. She looked at him with her one good eye and dropped her head again. "Sam . . ."

"Get up. Get ready. We're getting out of here."

"Oh, God. Sam?" For the first time, there was animation and comprehension in her voice. "Really you?"

"Please get up. No time to waste." He had to kill Kelly now, should have done it with the knife immediately. Concho would have. He moved forward toward Kelly, deciding how to do it. It would be in cold blood, but he was more than capable of that now, would enjoy it. He made his decision, dropped one hand to the knife in his belt. "Turn around," he said in a dry, harsh voice.

For the first time, there was a flicker of fear in Kelly's eyes. Behind Ramsey, the bed creaked. Nora was trying to stand up. "Sam," she said. "Drunk. Sorry. So drunk . . ."

Then, from behind, her full weight fell against Ramsey. Desperately clutching, she caught his gun arm, hung on.

Sheep Kelly was like a panther. One raised hand swooped down behind his head, came up holding a knife, and in almost the same motion, he dived for Ramsey. With all his muscle, Ramsey whipped his gun arm upward; he heard the bed groan as Nora fell back on it. He rammed his knife hand out to stop Kelly's charge, but the man was expecting that, writhed past it, and as his weight slammed into Ramsey, knocking him back, Ramsey felt the slash of Kelly's blade along the rind of meat over his ribs, and desperately he got the gun around and pulled the trigger, embracing Kelly with the other arm.

The body against his jerked; Ramsey fired again and again. The weight he held went limp, with a long, hissing sigh as if the air had gone out of it, and there was a clink as Kelly's knife fell to the floor. Ramsey let go and Kelly's body followed it, sagging, then sprawled sideways, blood staining all the left flank of his dirty underwear. But, Ramsey thought bitterly, the damage had been done, the alarm given.

There was no time to worry about that, nor about his failure to spot the knife sheath Kelly had worn down his back, Mexican-style, suspended from that silver chain. Ramsey whirled and found Nora sitting on the bed, staring dazedly through the haze of powder smoke; she sat there in a stupor, blinking. He jerked her up and slipped his arm around her, under her arms. "Come on," he grated. "We gotta get the hell outa here!"

She was almost dead weight, but not quite. In the front room she planted her feet. "Sam," she gasped. "Sick . . ." There was the splattering sound of vomit and its reek, as her body convulsed under his grasp. Ramsey stood helplessly for a full two minutes, and he could hear shouting outside now. Groggy men, awakened from sleep, were trying to find the source of the shots. It would not take them long.

Then, with a shuddering sigh, Nora raised her head. "Better," she gasped. "Sam, it's really you?"

"It's me. Come on." Her legs actually worked now as they moved toward the front door. Ramsey kicked it open, only to confront a man coming up the steps. "Sheep—" the man blurted, and then Ramsey shot him in the chest. The man went backwards off the porch. Ramsey moved out past the shelter of the door. All over the flat, lights were on, men ran about. Ramsey drew back, kicked something—Sheep Kelly's gun. He thrust his own, with only two rounds left, in his waistband, bent and scooped it up. They were trapped here in the house. Now it was up to Concho.

As if in answer to the thought, there was a faint, ripping sound from high up on the mountain. Then the night was full of neighing, whinnying, and horrible screaming. It almost drowned the burst–pause–burst of the machine gun.

Ramsey froze. "He's shooting the horses!" he cried. "Oh, goddam him, goddam Concho, he's shooting the horses!"

But it was their chance. The screaming mounted to a crescendo; he saw figures that had been heading for them turn toward the corral. He pulled Nora off the porch, caught her as she lurched, and then began to run, half dragging her with him. "It's that damn Lewis gun!" Somebody yelled above the screaming, and somebody else shrieked, "Lyman! Hey, Lyman!"

There were houses ahead of them, to their right, confused men boiling out their doors. Instinctively, they turned toward the racket at the corral, as Ramsey dragged the stumbling Nora to the left. The machine gun's sound was a steady ripping, now, and there were rifle flashes as people on the flat fired back. The horses were still screaming, and Ramsey cursed, thinking of Gibson Girl, Sunrise, the others— *Oh, goddam Concho, he didn't have to*—

Then the straw hat was spotted. One man, just emerged from a shack onto the starlit plain, paused, as his fellows ran on toward the mountain. "Hey, Lyman—!" he shouted. "What the hell's—" He ran toward Ramsey, halted, threw up his rifle. "You ain't Lyman!" he bawled, and Ramsey fired three shots at him from Kelly's gun at a distance of ten yards. The man reeled and fell, and the rifle went off wildly as he hit the ground.

Nora was running better now as they hurried on. Ramsey searched the blackness desperately for landmarks; they would have to circle right again to get to the horses. He looked behind him, saw the silhouettes of a half-dozen running men, in a kind of skirmish line headed toward the mountain. Then a strange thing happened; they all threw themselves down at once, hugging the ground, one of them cried out thickly, and the air was full of the whines of ricochets. Concho had raised his aim; he was no longer shooting at horses.

And now they were past the houses completely, out of that turmoil of confused combat. The machine gun seemed louder as they ran toward the foot of the mountain. Ramsey was getting winded; Nora's breathing was a series of tortured gasps. She stumbled, was dead weight. "Sam, can't run—"

Ramsey saw a shallow wash a few paces ahead of them.

He jerked her forward, pulled her down into its foot-deep depression, and covered her body with his own, as she retched dryly beneath him. Then from nowhere, the figure of a running man loomed almost above them. He carried a rifle. As Ramsey eared back the hammer of the Colt, the man leaped the ditch not two feet away and sped on towards the houses—a guard coming in. Ramsey watched him until he was a hundred yards past, then eased the hammer down.

He stood up, crouched low, and dragged Nora to her feet. They stumbled on, and Ramsey thought he knew where he was now. The machine-gun bursts on the mountain were shorter, terser; Concho's ammunition was running out.

They almost fell into the arroyo. It was deep, and it ran in the direction of the horses. Ramsey seized Nora and pulled her over the edge; they descended in a cloud of dust and gravel. At the bottom, he held her against him. "Not far now," he panted. "Can you go on?"

"Yes," she wheezed. "Sam, can't believe . . . thought you and Concho both dead. Oh, thank God." For a moment, she buried her face against his chest; Ramsey held her and watched the arroyo rim, but it was all worth it now, even the shooting of the horses. Then she raised her head. "Sorry . . . was so drunk. But Kelly hurt me so bad . . . If I'd known . . ."

"Forget it," he rasped. "Come on." With his arm about her, he led her down the arroyo. Behind them the character of the firing had changed; the machine gun could no longer be heard, only the sporadic rattle of rifle fire. While they ran, Ramsey punched fresh cartridges into his Colt, for Nora no longer constantly needed his support.

They stuck to the arroyo as long as Ramsey dared. Then they struggled up over its rim, and Ramsey knew for sure where he was now. The country was so broken, they could only jog-trot, but it offered cover and seemed deserted. The firing grew more distant.

Now Ramsey recognized the mouth of a draw. He pulled Nora into it, and they ran along its twisting length, its banks rising above them. Suddenly, as they rounded a bend, Ramsey halted, threw up the gun. Like a ghost, a giant black shape had materialized in front of them.

"Hold yo' fire!" Concho's voice snapped; and Ramsey saw that Concho had a rifle pointed at him. Then the Negro's voice changed. "Did you git her?"

"Concho!" Nora gasped. She pulled away from Ramsey and staggered forward.

"Noracita! Oh, thank God." Concho's voice trembled, and his long arms went about her and he held her tightly against him for a moment. Then he released her, and Ramsey strode forward and took her arm. Concho's voice was sharp. "Kelly. Whut about him?"

"He's dead," Ramsey snapped, suddenly full of a strange rage. "Goddammit, did you have to shoot the horses?"

"Why leave 'em somethin' to chase us with? 'Sides, when them lights come on, I had to do somethin'. Couldn't rake them houses for fear of hittin' y'all."

"The corral was full of my Morgans," Ramsey said bitterly.

"Tough." Concho turned away. "Wish we had one of 'em, now, though. We gonna hafta ride double." They followed him up the draw a dozen paces until the shapes of the horses became visible in the darkness. "Nora, you git up in front of Ramsey. I'll come along behind and take care of anybody might have a notion to follow us." He unslung one of the two rifles on his back and handed it to Ramsey. "Here's yo' Springfield, still loaded. Now, let's move out, while they still up on the mountain swarmin' over that machine-gun nest . . ."

* CHAPTER ELEVEN *

They made the best time they could under cover of darkness, but not enough. The country was rough and broken, the horses had been too long without good graze and sufficient water, and the one Ramsey and Nora rode grunted sullenly under their combined weight. Ramsey held the reins, his arms about Nora, and in the darkness she leaned back against him. She still smelled of cheap whiskey and vomit, but her hair, under Ramsey's nose, had a clean fragrance. Neither spoke; she was still groggy and suffering; he was content to hold her like that.

Just before dawn, Concho had them pull up. "Nora, how you makin' it?"

"I'll live," she said with a touch of gallows humor in her voice.

"We better swap hawses," Concho said. "Give that 'un a rest." He glanced at the sky. "Be light in a minute er two. I'm gonna climb that butte and take a look at our backtrail." He faded away up a hill like a wreath of morning mist.

On the ground, Nora leaned against Ramsey. "Sam, I'm so

damned ashamed of myself. After what you went through to get to me, finding me . . . drunk as a pig."

"Forget it," Ramsey said. "It's all over. Just forget it ever happened." He held her tightly. "A couple more days and maybe we'll be out of this devil's country."

"Oh, God, will we ever?" Nora said. "I hope I never see it again."

The sun rose with amazing speed; light flooded the badlands almost as if someone had flipped a switch. Ramsey jerked around as Concho came sliding back down the hill.

His dust-powdered face wore a grin. "No sign of them. They still runnin' around like ants in a stepped-on hill. I bet—" He broke off as, for the first time, he saw Nora's face in full light. The grin faded, and he strode forward and cupped her chin in his hand. "Lemme look at you," he rasped. Then he turned to Ramsey, eyes lambent. "Kelly did that?"

Ramsey nodded.

Concho drew in a deep breath. "How'd he die?"

"He jumped me," Ramsey said. "I shot him three times."

"I knowed I should have gone," Concho said in a terrible voice. "I'da rammed a rag in his mouth and spent about a half hour killin' him slow."

"It's all right, Concho," Nora said, turning her face away. "It'll heal." She took a step away from Ramsey. "Kelly didn't do anything to me that hadn't been done before."

Ramsey faced Concho. "The main thing," he said sharply, "is that it's over. We ain't talkin' about it any more, you understand? It's over."

Concho's eyes locked with his. Then understanding came into them. "Yeah," he said. "You right." He took a canteen from the saddle and turned to Nora. "Honey." His voice was gentle. "Don't you wanta take a little of this water and clean yourself up?"

Nora disappeared behind a clump of brush. Concho turned back to Ramsey, his eyes half-hooded. "Listen," he said in a low voice, "lemme tell you somethin'. That gal's all rattled. Husband killed right before her eyes, not two weeks 'go, then abused by that hawg Kelly . . . She ain't in no condition right now to think straight, you remember that. You took her away from Kelly, natch'lly she gonna be grateful for that. But that don't mean—"

Ramsey said, slowly and distinctly, "Concho, you mind your own goddam business."

"Nora is my business," Concho whispered savagely, and there was savagery, too, in his eyes. "Don't you ever fergit that for one minnit, friend."

Before Ramsey could answer, Nora appeared from behind

101

the bushes. She had rinsed her mouth, washed her face, and unsnarled the worst of the tangles in her hair. She halted and looked at the two men standing face to face, and then she said, in a clear voice, "I feel a lot better now. Hadn't we better ride on?"

Slowly, Concho's taut body relaxed. His eyes met Ramsey's one last time; then he turned away. "All right, Noracita," he said gently. "Come, I give you a leg up."

Nora suggested riding for the burned ranch, watering the horses there, and resting for the day in the cave, but Concho vetoed that. "That ranch a spot that draw down the lightnin'," he said, and he told her how they had got the horses. "It ain't Sheep Kelly's outfit I worried about no more; they bound to be all disorganized. Right now, they probably quarrelin' over who's in charge with Sheep daid. Whut we got to look out for is Mescans, Leon Sanchez' bunch. He got Yaqui trailers that can foller a fly across a glass window, and they gonna be lookin' for them two men I shot. They bound to trace 'em far as the ranch."

"Which way we head, then?" Ramsey asked.

"Due north. Git out of this territory fast as we can. On top of ever'thing else, they bound to heard that shootin' last night, they'll be ridin' over from San Vicente and Boquillas to see what it all about. They be thick as fleas down here; we got to git clear 'fore we run into 'em."

Ramsey said, "We're American citizens on American soil—"

Concho laughed, a short and ugly sound. "And on Mescan horses we killed two greasers to git."

"If they take us," Ramsey said, "these horses came out of Sheep Kelly's corral. Don't anybody forget that."

"They ain't gonna take us if we make tracks," Concho said. He lashed his horse with the reins. "Let's git outa here!"

They pushed the animals as hard as they dared, traveling now across high desert, tabletop flat, cutting, Concho said, for the old Comanche Trail north. The horses lathered badly, went grudgingly. Unless they got more than the pint of water each he and Concho had spared them from the canteen, they weren't going to last, Ramsey knew. But he also knew that every mile they could make right now meant that much more safety, and he pushed his weary mount ruthlessly.

Nora was a good rider; hands on the horn, she leaned back in Ramsey's encircling arms and was even able to talk at the pace they struck.

"Sam, I'm sorry," she said.

"Sorry about what?"

"That you didn't get back your horses."

His arms tightened about her. "Forget the horses," he said thickly.

"But you said they were all you had. What will you do now—when you get back to North Wells?"

"My ranch is free and clear. I've got a little savin's. Take that, put a mortgage on the place, buy some stock and start over."

"Start over," Nora said. "That has a wonderful sound to it. You're so lucky to be able to say it."

It was a moment before Ramsey answered. Then he said, "You can say it, too."

Nora only laughed, a strange sound with a metallic ring. "There's a lot you don't know about me, Sam Ramsey."

"A lot I do, too."

He felt her body stiffen. "What do you mean?"

He told her about Concho's delirium. "I know where Stewart found you and how you got there."

"Oh, God," she said with hopelessness. And then she said, resignedly, "Well, you were bound to find out." That brassy sound came back to her voice. "Don't you feel like a fool, risking your life for someone like me?"

"Shut up!" Ramsey said fiercely. "I told you it was over. Not only with Kelly. All of it."

"You don't understand," she said. "I ruin everything I touch. Poor Hank . . . Even that swine Kelly's dead because of me . . . Everything. I should have stayed in Baton Rouge. Maybe I'll go back there."

"No, you won't," Ramsey said. "We're going to North Wells."

A kind of shiver rippled over her body. Then she said, "You're forgetting something."

"What?"

"Concho," Nora said.

Ramsey was silent for a moment. Then he said, "He's in love with you. I don't mean *loves* you. I mean *in love* with you."

"Which is a crime, of course." There was an edge to Nora's voice.

"All right," Ramsey said. "It's none of my business."

She was silent for a moment. Then she said, "Yes, it is. I know what you're thinking. But it's not true, Sam. In my whole life, only three men have been kind to me—Hank Stewart, you, and Concho. And of all three, he's the only one that couldn't hope to gain anything by it."

"I see," Ramsey murmured.

"Sam—" She tried to turn in the saddle. At that moment, behind them, there was a yell from Concho. Ramsey reined

103

around. Concho was gesturing toward the south. A long plume of dust arose to stain the morning sky.

"Riders!" Concho bawled. "Mescans!" He gestured toward the west, where, a few miles distant, the Chisos Mountains reared their blue bulk amidst broken country, like a fortress. "Ride for cover!"

Cursing, Ramsey reined the protesting horse around. He saw now why the Mexican whose boots he wore had also worn the big-roweled spurs. Break a horse's spirit and you had to torture it to make it give all it had. But he'd discarded those spurs; now he lashed the tired and laboring animal with the reins.

The dust had peeled out from behind a range of buttes; now it widened its front. Ten, fifteen riders, Ramsey guessed. The horse was running better now; he locked Nora in his arms to hold her steady. Maybe they could make the Chisos, with the headstart they had—but what then? They could stand the Mexicans off for a while, but unless they could fort up where there was water— He quit thinking, bending every effort to get the last ounce of speed out of the foaming horse.

Only three miles, four; surely the horse could make it. But the dust was closing fast. The Mexicans' mounts were fresh, well-fed, well-watered. Already, craning his head over his shoulder, he could see, through shimmering heat waves, the actual forms of riders in the van of the dust cloud.

Mercilessly, he lashed and kicked the horse. Beneath his legs, its flanks pumped like bellows. He was intensely alert to the rhythm of its pounding hoofs, dreading any faltering. They soared across shallow dry washes, crashed through creosote. Nora was holding tightly to the horse's mane and the saddle horn. Behind, Concho had to rein in to keep from passing them.

The Chisos were closer now. Two miles would see them in country where there was at least a chance to find cover. Their vast, blue bulk blotted out the sky.

And then the horse faltered, stumbled, almost fell, and broke into an awkward, limping trot.

Ramsey knew immediately what had happened, and his heart sank. He passed the reins to Nora, swung down, and as Concho pulled up, Ramsey was already lifting the animal's forefoot.

"What happened?" Concho yelled, veins standing out on his forehead.

"Threw a goddam shoe!" It dangled from a single bent nail. The animal had been cold-shod, the nails not properly clenched. The hoof was split and maimed. Ramsey cursed and wrenched the last nail out, flung the shoe away and let the horse's foot drop. Then he turned and pulled Nora from the saddle.

"Git up in front of Concho!" he rasped. "He knows this country." He unslung the Springfield, loosened the blanket roll in which spare cartridges were stored. "I'll slow them down."

"No! They'll kill you, Sam!"

"Goddam it, don't argue. Take her, Concho!" Ramsey wrestled her over to the Negro's mount. She kicked and squirmed savagely. "No, Sam!" she cried. "Please, don't—"

Concho swung down, his massive arm encircling her. He looked at Ramsey strangely. Then he said, slowly, almost sadly, "You two go on. Head between them two mountains yonder; there's water there." He reached for Ramsey's blanket roll. "I'll shoot this lame critter and fort up behind him. I wish I had Kelly's Lewis gun now."

There was no time to argue. Ramsey shoved Nora to Concho's horse. "Git up!" he snapped.

But suddenly, with amazing strength, she wrenched away from him. She grabbed one of the extra rifles from its boot. "No!" she snapped, breasts heaving beneath the denim jacket. "Damn it, I can shoot, too. With three good rifles against them—"

Ramsey struck down the gun. "Don't be a fool. There's no cover!" At that moment, Concho's horse grunted, lurched. Simultaneously, Ramsey heard the distant bark of a rifle. Slowly, as if it were very weary, the horse sagged down, then fell over.

It had been between them and the riders. Now Ramsey could see a man in the forefront mounting up again, rifle in his hand. The dust cloud came on, at a slower pace, and Concho said, savagely, "Well, that's that." His hand shoved at Nora's shoulder. "Git down behind that dead hawse, girl!"

"No, Concho," Ramsey said quietly and he tossed his Springfield away. Then he reached over and took the rifle from Nora and threw it after his own.

Concho stared at him. "You outa your mind?"

Ramsey was unbuckling his cartridge belt. "You're out of yours," he said. "You want to get Nora shot? We can't fight and we can't run. All we can do is surrender.

"Raise your hands," Ramsey said to Nora. "High." He did the same, as she slowly, hesitantly, obeyed.

Concho's voice faltered. "They'll shoot us down where we stand."

"Maybe not, if we don't give 'em any reason."

"Sam's right, Concho," Nora said, her voice actually relieved, as if glad to have the issue settled. "It's the only thing we can do."

Concho looked from one to the other. Then he said, "But you don't know Sanchez." He let out a long, shuddering breath. Sun glinted off the weapons and gear of the oncoming Mexicans. "Hell," he said, "it's too late now," and disgustedly he tossed the Springfield aside, unbuckled his gun belt, and raised his own hands.

And that was how they were standing when the band of Mexicans came up.

There were twelve of them—dressed in a mixture of peon garb, khaki uniforms, and *charro* clothes. Their leader rode a gray horse. He was clad in an ornate sombrero, a khaki shirt crisscrossed with gleaming cartridge bandoliers, and *charro* pants that were skin-tight and emblazoned with braid. When he reined in, the gray horse reared. Behind him, eleven carbines were trained on Nora, Ramsey, and Concho. The leader dismounted.

He walked toward them with something of the strut of a rooster, not a tall man, all wide-shouldered torso and short, bowed, rider's legs. He stopped six feet away, put his hands on his lean hips, and his big spurs jingled as he planted his feet wide apart. He stared at them with narrowed black eyes in a square, very dark, flat-nosed face.

For a moment or two, the silence of the morning was unbroken, except for the sound of the riders forming a circle around them. Then the man in front of them said, *"Hola,* Concho."

For the first time that Ramsey could remember, there was fear in Concho's voice. "Fierro!"

The Mexican tipped back his sombrero. He was smiling. It was the smile of a wolf about to take a lamb. *"Si.* A long time, *no es verdad?"*

"What are you doing here?" Concho's Spanish was flawless. Ramsey, who had only the mongrel border Spanish, was startled.

"On a mission for Francisco," Fierro said. "The campaign in Coahuila had not been pursued with sufficient aggressiveness. I shall remedy that." He looked at Ramsey and the woman. "Who are your friends, and how is it that you ride horses of Sanchez?"

"I know nothing of horses of Sanchez," Concho said.

"Our trackers, who are Yaqui Indians and without compare, recognized the shoes. Two of Sanchez' men are missing, and last night there was much shooting by Mariscal Moun-

106

tain, and now we find you and these gringos on Sanchez' horses. How did this happen?"

"We caused the shooting at Mariscal," Concho said. "The American bandit, Kelly—"

"Not bandit. Sympathizer with our cause."

"The American bandit, Kelly, had taken the wife of another man, this woman. We took her back and killed Kelly. We escaped on two horses from his corral—these."

"Killed Kelly?" Fierro's brows went up. "The two of you?"

"Yes," Concho said. "After we took his Lewis gun—"

"I thought I recognized the technique of the firing. Incredible. Still the old Concho, always ready to spit in the devil's eye." Fierro's gaze went to the other horse, standing with raised forefoot. He walked over to it, gripped its pastern, glanced at the hoof. Then he pulled a .38 Smith & Wesson from his sash, put it behind the animal's ear, and pulled the trigger. The horse crashed to the ground. As if the conversation had not been interrupted, Fierro said, "I am impressed that you wear no guns, Concho. As you grow older, you gather wisdom." He gestured with his own revolver. "Now, you will each mount ahead of one of my men."

Ramsey said, "Where are you taking us?"

"Across the Rio Bravo," Fierro said. "To Boquillas. There to meet General Sanchez, whose territory this is. Together, he and I will hear your story and decide what disposition is to be made of you." He jerked the revolver again. *"Andale!* We must ride!"

★   ★   ★

Under guard, they rode a long way through the desert, down the dry, winding bed of Tornillo Creek, and thence to the head of Boquillas Canyon. Mounted ahead of a Mexican as silent as if carved from stone, Ramsey felt the constant pressure of a pistol barrel against his body the whole way. As for Concho, he was the center of a whole clot of guards. Nora had been given a horse to herself; at the lead, Fierro rode almost thigh to thigh with her. There was never the slightest chance of escape.

It was midafternoon when they reached the Boquillas ford of the Rio. All about them towered painted cliffs and buttes. On the American side, there was a scatter of empty adobe houses, an abandoned settlement whose only inhabitant was an American whom the Mexicans had not bothered because he was already dying of tuberculosis. A human wraith, he stood outside his hut and watched curiously as the cavalcade filed down to the river.

At the ford, the water was not hock-deep to the horses. On the Mexican side, atop a high plateau, was a village, consisting of a dozen adobe huts scattered around a wide, dusty, unornamented plaza. Behind the town loomed the huge, striated wall of the great escarpment of the del Carmens. Half-naked children and a motley assortment of pigs, dogs, and chickens played in the sunshine. When the column entered the plaza, people suddenly filled the doorways of the huts, and the children ran forward, shouting with wonder and excitement.

In the center of the plaza, Fierro raised his hand and the detachment halted. Fierro barked an order that Ramsey did not catch, then swung down. Spurs jingling, he strode through the door of what was apparently the town's cantina. No one else dismounted. Nor did the pressure of the gun barrel against Ramsey ease.

Then Fierro reappeared. "Bring them in!" he shouted. The man behind Ramsey slid down and gestured with the revolver. Ramsey dismounted. A Mexican was helping Nora from the saddle. The three of them were herded together and marched across the plaza. As they went, Concho said, "Fierro. Dammit, why did he have to be here?"

"Who is he?" Ramsey asked.

"Pancho Villa's right-hand man. He's also the damnedest butcher that ever walked in boots." Concho spat. "And he hates my guts."

"Good God," Ramsey said, something clicking in his brain. His heart sank. *Rodolfo* Fierro?"

"That's him," Concho said.

The newspaper reports came back to Ramsey now. There had been protest in America about Villa's cold-blooded mass slaughter of captured federal troops and sympathizers in each town he won from the government. Without trial or mercy, they were murdered by the hundred. And Rodolfo Fierro was Villa's executioner, a bloodthirsty weasel of a man who killed for the love of it. No wonder Concho had been afraid—

Then they were pushed into the dim coolness of the cantina. It had two small rooms, a bar in the front one, a pool table in the other. Behind a table near the bar sat a lanky man with skin the color of coffee with cream. His lean face was like a blade, his eyes hooded and dark. He wore a general's blue dress-coat with golden epaulets and khaki pants thrust into cavalry boots. A bottle of tequila sat before him; Rodolfo Fierro stood beside him.

"This is General Leon Sanchez, Commander of the Army of Northern Coahuila," Fierro said. "Your names, please."

"Concho Platt," Concho said. It was the first time Ramsey

had heard his last name. Then Concho said, "General, you know me. You know I served with Villa, too—"

Sanchez cut him off with a raised hand. He was looking at Nora. For the first time, light flickered in his eyes. *"Senora* Stewart." He shifted his gaze to one of his men. "You will bring the senora a chair!" he snapped. He arose and bowed. "Welcome to our humble headquarters." His English was good, though heavily accented.

"Hello, General Sanchez," Nora said.

"And you." Sanchez looked at Ramsey.

"Sam Ramsey. I'm a rancher from North Wells."

Sanchez nodded. Fierro said, "With your permission, *Don* General. May I question these *Yanquis?*"

Sanchez shrugged and poured a glass of tequila. Fierro said to Ramsey, "You will now tell us your whole story."

"Well, it's this way." Ramsey spoke in a mixture of Spanish and English; the two officers listened closely. "Sheep Kelly stole my herd of Morgans and I came in here to get them." He related events substantially as they had happened, except that he omitted all mention of Concho's ambush of the two Mexicans and told the lie they had agreed on. "I opened the corral, took these two horses and their gear. We didn't know they belonged to your men."

Fierro's eyes bored into his. "For a horseman, you did not choose wisely."

"It was dark," Ramsey said, returning his gaze steadily. "There was a lot of shooting. No time to pick."

"And strangely, both horses turned out to be from our band." Fierro's mouth twitched wickedly, and he also poured a glass of tequila. Before he drank it, he spinkled salt on the back of his hand. "Remarkable."

Sanchez spoke then. "You have done us a serious disservice. You have killed Kelly, and he was valuable to us; he kept our army supplied."

"He shouldn't have taken my horses or the woman," Ramsey said. "If they'd been Mexican horses, a Mexican woman, a Mexican would have killed him. You give us Americans credit for less *machismo?*"

"Still," Sanchez said, "you have committed a serious crime against the Revolutionary Army and against General Villa."

"Listen, Sanchez," Concho said. "You know I fought with Villa against Diaz in the old days, with Madero."

Fierro smiled. "Madero's dead."

"It makes no difference. I was a colonel. Villa won't have forgotten me."

"Then perhaps he will light a candle for you," Fierro said.

Concho jerked up his head and looked at Fierro.

Fierro went on, his voice silky. "General Villa now has almost a hundred thousand men under arms, my friend, even a force of flying machines. Do you think he worries about one black ex-colonel? I can assure you he does not. I have shot better friends of Villa than you, Concho, at his command."

Concho's temper slipped its leash. "Why, you two-bit—!" he flared in English, but Ramsey's voice cut him off.

Ramsey looked at Sanchez. "General Sanchez," he said, "there's one thing everybody here seems to have forgotten. We're American citizens. You took us on American soil."

Sanchez said, "So?"

"I think you'd better forget this talk of shooting." Ramsey's voice was full of a confidence he did not feel. "If anything happens to us, you'll be in damned bad trouble with the United States Government—and so will General Villa."

Fierro made a contemptuous sound in his throat, but the hoods on Sanchez' eyes lifted. He leaned back in his chair and looked at Ramsey without expression. "Go on," he said.

"There's a lot of sympathy for Villa in the United States," Ramsey went on desperately, but keeping the desperation out of his voice. "He buys horses, guns, ammunition on our side of the border—hell, Americans even took moving pictures of his campaigns last year. When Americans landed at Vera Cruz, he refused to go down there and fight 'em. And the way I understand it, he's issued strict orders that all American citizens in Mexico are to be treated with respect and left unharmed. Now, if anything happens to us and it ruins Villa's relations with the United States, who's he going to blame for it?"

Suddenly he realized he'd scored a point. Something flickered, shifted in Sanchez' eyes; he turned to Fierro inquiringly. Fierro spat on the floor of the cantina.

"Listen, *Yanqui*," he said. "I'm General Villa's personal representative here. What I order done is to be done as if he ordered it himself."

"Nevertheless," Sanchez said, and now his voice was dubious. "Nevertheless—"

Fierro slammed the table with a clenched fist. The tequila bottle jumped. *"I command for Villa here!"* He straightened up and he was panting, his eyes actually glowed red. "You will not tell me," he rasped through clenched teeth, "how I shall command!"

Sanchez shoved back his chair and stood up. "General Fierro, you *represent* Villa. It is I, Leon Sanchez, who commands."

Fierro's chest swelled, but his voice was under control when he spoke again. "I thought you had understood my po-

110

sition, General Sanchez. I am here as Francisco Villa's personal representative. And as such, you will respond to my orders." He looked at Ramsey and Concho with mindless hatred. "These *Yanquis*"—he spat the word—"have disrupted your supply line. They were taken riding the horses of your two missing men. I charge them with murder and interference with the Revolution." He turned on his heel and gestured toward the other room. "Come, we will confer."

For a moment, it seemed that Sanchez would refuse. He stood there indecisively. Then, as Fierro led the way, he followed. Moving to the far corner of the other room, they talked in low, intense voices, words indistinguishable. But their hands moved choppily, angrily. They were like two fighting cocks, Ramsey thought, face to face just before the pitting. And he knew now that their lives hung on which one of them won . . .

He took a step forward, despite the guards, and put his hand on Nora's shoulder. There was nothing he could say, and he said nothing. She turned and looked up at him, and the part of her face not bruised was chalk-white. But, incredibly, she managed a faint smile, and she raised her hand and put it on his.

"That damn Fierro," Concho grunted. "I wish I'd killed the bastard when I had the chance, years ago. We took a town and he shot the mayor. I knocked the little sonofabitch sidewinding before he could shoot the mayor's wife and three little kids and stomped on him to make sure he was out of action for a while. Pancho backed me up, too, and Fierro ain't forgot no part of it . . ."

"Silence!" snapped one of the guards. He rammed Concho in the back with a gun muzzle.

Ramsey watched the conversation come to an end in the other room. And his lips thinned as he saw that Sanchez' hands had fallen to his sides, while Fierro was still gesturing. Then Fierro grinned and clapped Sanchez on the back. The two men turned and came back to where the prisoners stood waiting. Fierro swaggered a little, his gold-toothed smile wide. Sanchez walked stiffly, his face somber, his lips compressed.

Nora's hand tightened on Ramsey's. Fierro looked at them and his smile was like a skull's. "Well, my friends," he said, "you have been tried and found guilty of interference with the Revolution. The two men will be executed by a firing squad immediately." His eyes flickered over Nora. "We shall make other disposition of the *senora*. We do not make war on women."

✳   ✳   ✳

111

"Oh, no," Nora whispered. "No, please—"

"You jackel," Concho said. "When Villa finds out about this—"

"We do not bother our *Jefe* with small details," Fierro smirked. "He will not find out."

"Villa finds out everything," Concho said, and his eyes swung to Sanchez. "They used to say in the mountains that Pancho Villa could hear the cactus grow."

"It will grow very thick over your graves," Fierro said. He gestured. "Take them away."

A guard wrenched at Concho. Nora sprang to her feet. "No!" she screamed. "No, you can't shoot them! They're Americans—We—"

Sanchez lifted an ineffectual hand. Fierro said harshly, advancing to Nora, his eyes boring into hers, "Be quiet, woman."

Nora's voice trailed off. Suddenly, quite without warning, she spat full into Fierro's face. "You pig," she said, softly and with utter contempt. "You dirty greaser pig. You can't make me stay with you. I don't stay with dirty greaser pigs."

Fierro's face did not change. He lifted a hand, then let it drop and dragged his sleeve across his spittle-wet face. "Very well," he said. "I don't need a filthy *Yanqui* slut." He jerked his head. "Take her with the others."

Nora smiled insolently. "The *Yanqui* slut spits in your face," she said, and did it again, and Fierro's hand dropped toward his .38. Concho started to spring; a guard rammed a rifle barrel into his belly, blocking him; another stepped in front of Ramsey.

Fierro's deeply indrawn breath was audible, a shuddering sound, in the silent room. Then he said quietly: "I shall command the firing squad myself. General Sanchez, you will accompany me?"

Sanchez made a sound in his throat, then nodded. Hemmed in by guards, Concho, Ramsey and Nora were pushed through the door and out into the blinding three o'clock sun. "Girl," Concho said despairingly, "why'd you do it? Now they'll kill you, too."

"Don't you think I knew that?" Nora said quietly. Then she said, "I'm tired of running. I'm tired of it all. I only wish—" She looked at Ramsey.

"Silence," a guard commanded.

"Go to hell," Ramsey said. They were being marched across the plaza, children capering alongside. Ahead of them were the ruins of a house gutted by fire, only its adobe walls still standing. He said, "Nora, I'm sorry. I should have given you and Concho horses at Double Springs, when we first met, let you ride on."

"It wouldn't have made any difference," Nora said. "You can't outrun what's going to happen to you. I don't blame you, Sam."

"Well, I blame myself," Ramsey said bitterly, full of impotent rage at his own helplessness to save her. If it would do her any good, he'd break, take on every soldier in this village single handed . . . But that would only hasten her own execution, too.

Now they had reached the side of the burned building. The *caporal* in charge of the guard detail barked an order. The prisoners were turned to face the wall, their hands jerked behind them. Ramsey felt ropes pulled tight around his wrist. Then they were jerked around and their backs rammed against the wall, Nora between the two men.

The guards moved away, ten yards, lounging with guns cradled in their arms. The *caporal* looked toward the cantina, but Sanchez and Fierro had not emerged yet.

"Sam," Nora said, "I'm afraid. My knees are weak."

Ramsey moved over. "Lean against me," he said.

She did, her weight on his flank. He felt the feathery brush of her hair against his cheek. "Sam," she said, "I don't know if it will make it any easier for you, but can I tell you something?"

"Yes."

"I love you," she said.

Ramsey sucked in a great breath. "I love you, too," he said. It was the first time he had said those words to any woman. They came with startling ease.

"That does make it better," Nora said shakily.

Concho made a sound in his throat. Ramsey turned his head. The Negro, standing very erect against the wall, was looking at them. His eyes glared with a hatred every bit equivalent to that he'd displayed for Fierro. His mouth was a hard, set line.

Nora straightened up. "Concho," she said softly. "Don't begrudge me this. Not this late in the game . . ."

Concho opened his mouth, then closed it. He looked straight ahead.

The *caporal* said: "Attention! The generals come!"

Sanchez and Fierro strode toward them across the plaza. Even at this distance, they could hear the jingling of Fierro's spurs. Ramsey swallowed hard down a dry throat and moved closer to Nora, wishing he could put his arm around her. Now the generals were within earshot; Sanchez was still talking, gesticulating. "I tell you, Fierro, this is more complicated than you think. If Villa hears, I will be the one—"

Fierro halted, lifted a hand. "Be silent," he rasped. Then he gestured. "There are two hundred and fifty kilometers of chaparral between ourselves and Villa. More than enough in which to hide three gringo corpses. Now, an end to it, the men mustn't hear—" Frowning, he strode on, Sanchez a pace behind.

The frown vanished as he confronted the prisoners. Again gold teeth showed in a wolfish smile. "Well, gringos, are you ready?" In reply, Concho spat.

Fierro stepped back. The guards arranged themselves in a rank. "Such men need no blindfolds," Fierro snapped. He turned his head toward the guards. "*Listo!*" They raised and aimed their rifles.

Ramsey gasped, "Steady, Nora."

She answered something, but he never heard it. Her words were drowned in the sudden frightened squawking of the chickens about their feet. The skinny fowl ran frantically, crouching low, cackling in fright. Across the plaza, a horse reared and neighed.

Suddenly Sanchez sprang forward. He yelled something at the guards, seized Fierro and spun him around, pointing upward. Ramsey raised his head, and then he saw it, too.

It came out of the westering sun, like an enormous hawk. Even above the squawking of the chickens, the braying of burros, the frightened whinnying of horses, they could hear the thin popping roar of its engine. Prisoners forgotten, the firing squad turned to stare.

"Whut the hell—" Concho blurted.

Hope sprang up in Ramsey. "It's an airplane!" he yelled. "It must be one of Villa's. They say he's got half a dozen!"

Dropping below the line of the great escarpment, the craft skimmed toward them over the plateau. As its shadow seemed to blot out the plaza, devour it, the village was in a turmoil. Animals plunged and ran, one of the guards crossed himself. Ramsey could see the pilot now, leather-clad, amidst a cat's cradle of wires and struts. Then, dropping ever lower, the airplane turned and sailed out across the desert.

"Oh, God, let it land," Ramsey grated.

Sure enough, it disappeared below the thickety rim of the chaparral. Fierro stared, frozen; then, in the midst of uproar, turned to the disorganized firing squad. "Fall in!" he shrieked. "You fools, back in ranks. We have business!"

"No!" Sanchez bellowed, breaking from his trance-like fascination with the landing aircraft. "Ground your arms! That is my order!"

Fierro's flat face was savage. "General Sanchez—"

"My order, you understand?" Cords stood out in Sanchez' neck. "The flyer of this thing has come from General Villa, and will return to him. Shall he report three dead Americans in my camp?" Sanchez whipped a pistol from its holster. "I'll kill the first man who shoots until I give the order!"

"Oh, God," Nora said, and sagged against Ramsey. He told himself, his own knees weak, *Count on nothing. In this country, count on nothing . . .*

Already, riders were thundering out of the plaza toward the place where the plane had landed. Women and children, shrieking with excitement, ran after them on foot. Sanchez, lowering his gun, drew a dagger from his sash. "Turn around," he said to Concho and began to saw at his bonds. Fierro rasped, "Sanchez, you fool—"

"Not fool enough to forget I command here and am responsible to Villa." The ropes parted, Sanchez moved on to Nora. Then, as he sliced Ramsey's bonds, he said, "You will not try to escape. What disposition will be made of you will be decided later. But if you try to escape, you will be shot." He was breathing hard, as if his moment of decision had cost him most of his strength.

Ramsey didn't even hear him. He had turned to Nora, gathered her into his arms. Soldiers moved in to ring them with pointed rifles.

Then, from the rim of the plateau, there was noise—an excited, fiesta chorus of shouts. Two riders appeared over the rim, and one of them, awkward in the saddle, was the leather-clad pilot of the airplane. As he came into the plaza, Ramsey saw with a kick of his heart that the man was an American.

"Hey, buddy!" Concho bellowed. "Hey, American, over here!"

The rider raised himself in his stirrups, sweeping back his goggles. Sanchez and Fierro strode toward him, but he rode past them, bouncing loosely in the saddle. He pulled up in front of Ramsey.

He was lanky, young, and had three days' beard. His face was smudged dark, and he reeked of castor oil. His pale-blue eyes swept over them, and he blurted: "What the hell?"

"Man!" Concho said jubilantly. "You got here jest in time! We was bein' 'dobe-walled!"

"The hell you say! Americans?"

Sanchez came trotting up, Fierro behind him. Sanchez said, breathlessly, "I am General Sanchez. I command here. You come from General Villa?"

"Yes. My name's Bill Weber. But what are these three

Americans doin' up against this wall? And a woman, too!" He looked down at Sanchez and his eyes were hard.

Fierro came up. "They have been tried and are being executed for crimes against the Revolution!" he snapped.

Weber stared at him blankly, then spat tobacco juice into the dust from an enormous cud in his cheek. "Aw, come off it, Fierro. You know Villa's orders about American citizens."

"These are guilty of special crimes!"

Weber swung down off the horse. "Listen, Fierro, nobody shoots an American in Villa's army without Pancho's personal okay, and you know that as good as I do. What are you up to, you bloodthirsty little—"

"You're insubordinate!" Fierro screamed. "I'll have you tried and executed!"

"You *do* that," Weber said, and he spat again. "Soon's you find somebody else knows how to fly." He turned to Sanchez. "General, I don't know what these folks have done, but if you value your hide, you won't harm 'em without Villa's written permission. You do, and you're liable to be 'dobe-walled yourself. The General don't want the American Army comin' in here after him."

Sanchez swallowed. "I assure you that there will be no violation of the General's orders in my command. Nevertheless, these people have committed serious crimes against us." He looked at Fierro. "However, in view of the General's orders, with which I was not familiar, perhaps it would be better if the sentence were not carried out. Instead, they shall be expelled from Mexico."

"Oh, Sam—" Nora buried her face against Ramsey's shoulder.

"That sounds better," Weber said. He turned to Ramsey. "I thought everybody from the silver mine had beat it back to the States."

"We're not from the silver mine. They picked us up in Texas and brought us across the Rio. I'm Sam Ramsey, this is Nora Stewart, Concho Platt."

Weber jerked his head around. "Concho? Not the same one that was with Villa against Diaz—?"

"That's me," Concho said.

"Judas Priest! Villa still talks about you and those damn machine guns." He grinned. "But I got a wilder racket than that. I fly over the *Federales* and drop hand-grenades on 'em. You oughta see what confusion *that* causes."

Sanchez said, almost pleadingly, *"Senor* Weber. You have orders for me—?"

"Yeah." Weber drew a packet from his coat. "Villa wants you in Torreon—a new offensive." He handed it to Sanchez.

116

"This is the most out-of-the-way spot in Mexico—that's why I brought 'em by plane. I understand there's some gasoline up at the silver mine; you better send somebody after it, because I'm gonna need it."

"That will be done!" For a moment, Ramsey thought Sanchez was going to salute. Then the Mexican turned away with the packet. Weber spat into the dust again.

"God, I'm dry," he said. "They got a drink in this town? I reckon folks that was almost shot could stand a drink. Anyhow, I got to hear your story. I'll have to make a full report to General Villa." Nora was crying, her face still buried against Ramsey. "Don't take on so, ma'am. You're gonna be all right. You got Bill Weber's word for it, and I rank just as high as any other general this side of Francisco Villa himself. You're gonna be just fine." He patted her shoulder awkwardly and looked at Ramsey. "Come on," he said. "I'm buyin'. Lord, it's been a long time since I've had a drink with Americans!"

★ CHAPTER TWELVE ★

Bill Weber, a South Carolinian, had built his own airplane and had taught himself to fly four years ago. Barnstorming around the country, giving rides and exhibitions, he'd wrecked his craft beyond repair in El Paso and, stranded, had responded to an offer from Villa, who had purchased a motley fleet of second-hand planes for use against the Government. "Flyin' that old Curtiss pusher for Pancho," Weber told them over beer in the cantina, "ain't what you'd call the way to a ripe old age, but it pays good. And since airmen don't grow on every bush, I draw a lot of water. That's why I can afford to cross Fierro, which generally ain't a wise idea. Even Pancho himself thinks twice before he does it." He signaled to the bartender to set up a round for the three guards who still surrounded the prisoners. "I might not have got away with it if Pancho really hadn't laid down the law about Americans. Anyhow, I'm gonna see to it that you git your guns back, food, water, and three horses. They got to bring gas down from the mine and I got some work to do on the kite, so I'll be here until late tomorrow. The sooner you can head out before then, the longer I'll be around to make sure that damned Fierro don't send nobody after you."

"We'll go soon as the horses are ready," Ramsey said.

"And ride like hell," Concho added.

"That's the ticket. You know somethin'? You're lucky Boquillas ain't got no telegraph, no post office, and that it's damn hard to reach on horseback. This plane was about the only way to git a message to Sanchez that wouldn't take two weeks." He pulled some envelopes from his jacket. "Speakin' of post offices, what about mailin' these for me when you git back to the States? I reckon the folks back home in Columbia think I'm dead by now."

Sam Ramsey took them. "Friend," he said fervently, "I'll even pay for the stamps."

Weber was as good as his word. The horses and equipment were ready in an hour—though what it cost in argument to get them must have been considerable. Weber shook hands with them after they were mounted. "Good luck," he said. "Now, hightail it while Sanchez and Fierro are still wavin' their hands at each other."

Nora leaned down from the saddle and kissed his forehead. Then they galloped across the plaza, down the slope of the plateau, through the willows and reeds along the river, crossed the ford, with Concho in the rear, hand on his gun, head craned back over his shoulder; and then they were back on American soil.

From then on, they pushed the horses without mercy, pausing for an hour's guarded rest only when they struck water. Always, either Ramsey or Concho was on lookout for the remnants of Sheep Kelly's band or any pursuit from across the Rio. But they pushed all the way up the dry bed of Tornillo Creek without seeing another rider. Where it crossed the old Comanche war trail, they left it and rode hard, due north, toward Persimmon Gap, the main pass through the Santiagos. Once Concho thought he saw a horseman on a distant butte and they unsheathed their rifles, but the rider vanished and never reappeared.

Then they were through the mountains, so weary that they reeled in their saddles. Mile by tortuous mile, the last of the desert fell behind them. At last they were clear of it, in the high grasslands, and now, finally, it was safe to relax. They reined in and looked behind them at the long, blue barrier of the Santiagos, shimmering in the distance, and Concho let out a long whistling breath. "We made it," he said.

"Thank God," Nora said, voice trembling.

Ramsey stared at that shimmering wasteland and had the sensation of waking from a nightmare. He looked at Nora and for a moment she seemed unreal, only something out of that tortured dream. Then he edged his mount closer, put out a hand and touched her, and her eyes met his, and there was no more unreality. He had gone down into deep Big Bend and come back with a woman. As her hand closed over his, he knew the trip had been worth it.

Concho's voice sliced through the moment, harshly. "No time fer lollygaggin'. Let's git on." The Negro pulled his horse around and kicked it savagely.

Late in the afternoon of the third day, their straining horses topped a rise. Below them lay miles of good grassland, and, near at hand, a scatter of buildings, corrals, and a slowly turning windmill.

Ramsey swallowed hard, pulling up his horse. "There it is," he said, gesturing. "That's my place."

Nora stood up in her stirrups. "Oh, Sam," she whispered. "It's beautiful."

Ramsey's eyes swept the empty pastures. It would take a long time to fill them again. But that did not matter now. "Let's go down," he said.

Homecoming. Ramsey showed Nora through the house, proudly, glad that he had kept everything meticulously neat and in repair, and she exclaimed delightedly over it all, while Concho stalked along behind them, silently, a huge, black shadow.

Not until Nora had seen everything, even to examining the cookstove and checking the inventory of the food safe, did their fatigue hit them. Then it came like the hammer-blow of a fist, and when Ramsey saw Nora sway, he caught her and eased her down into a chair at the kitchen table. Then he felt his own weariness.

The indestructible Concho looked at them with contempt. "I'll see to the hawses," he grunted and strode out.

Nora gave a long, shuddering sigh. "Oh, Sam, I can hardly believe it. To be safe again, in a place like this—"

Ramsey touched her hand. "You can believe it," he said. His voice was soft. "You're safe and I'm gonna keep you that way." Then, wearily, he stood up. "Come on," he said, took her hand, and led her into the other room. There was a trunk in one corner, and he unlocked it. "These clothes," he said, "were my mother's. I know they're all outa style, and we'll buy you new stuff in North Wells. But for right now, maybe you can find something in here you can use. She was about your size."

Nora dropped to her knees by the trunk, lifted out the crisp but faded garments. "Anything," she whispered. "Anything clean . . . This and this and this." Then she froze,

119

looking up at him. Her eyes were embarrassed. "Sam," she murmured, "after what I've been . . . You're sure you want me to wear her clothes?"

Ramsey nodded. "I'm sure," he said. He helped her to her feet. "There's a shower out back."

He had expected a transformation in her, but not that much of one. A half hour later, when she came in through the back door of the kitchen, Ramsey, turning away from the stove, gaped.

The swelling in her face had gone down over the past few days; her eyes were normal and only the faintest suspicion of a bruise remained on her cheek. She was clean-scrubbed and glowing, her chestnut hair a long, glittering, damp fall down her back. She wore a frilly white blouse that had belonged to his mother, a flowered skirt, and sandals. Refreshed, free of fear, vibrant with happiness . . . he saw her as he had never seen her before, and he whispered, "My God, you're beautiful." Then he took her in his arms and kissed her, and she held him tightly and returned the kiss hungrily.

The back door slammed; Concho entered. "Hawses rubbed down and—" he broke off. Then he said, softly: "How long Hank Stewart been dead now? Two weeks?"

Nora turned. "Oh, Concho—"

"Never mind," Concho said in a voice of contempt. He turned and went out again, the door slamming once more.

Nora pulled away, and the light that had made her glow died. Ramsey said harshly, angrily, "Forget it—"

Dully, Nora said, "I don't know what to do. I just don't know what to do."

Ramsey reached for her again, but she eluded his grasp. Not looking at him, she went to the stove. "You'll want to get cleaned up, Sam. I'll finish the cooking. It's woman's work, anyhow."

Nora sliced a country ham, fried it, cooked rice with peppers and stewed canned tomatoes. Delicious as it was, the meal was eaten in silence, partly because their hunger was so great the three of them wolfed their food, but mostly because of the tension that settled over the table the moment Concho took his seat.

When every dish was cleaned, the silence persisted. Then Concho took out makings and began to roll a cigarette. As he licked it, his eyes met Ramsey's, and there was ugliness in them. Concho rammed the smoke between his lips, lit it, and let blue vapor trail from his nostrils. "Now," he said. "We got one problem left. Them men that hanged Hank Stewart."

Nora sat straight, her hands lacing and unlacing nervously. "Well?" Concho snapped.

Her voice was shaky. "Concho, we've already had so much trouble—"

"Then a little more won't hurt. He was your husband, woman, and he fresh in his grave."

"Concho, please. Won't you try to understand? We—"

"I understand this man make us a promise. He say, if we turn around, go back down into deep Big Bend with him, he sic the law on them men that hanged yo' husband."

"But Hank's dead!" Nora's voice rose. "And making more trouble won't bring him back! Sam's told you—those men that killed him are the most powerful in this county. If he sets himself against them—"

Concho slammed the table and shoved back his chair. "He was yo' husband, Noracita! You sittin' here now in a nice clean kitchen in nice clean clothes. But where you think you be now if he hadn't married you out of that place? You forgot where you was—?"

"I haven't forgotten!" Nora screamed. "But I've been through enough, can't you understand? I've had all I can take, I don't want any more, I can't stand any more—"

Concho got to his feet. "Okay," he said flatly. "Well, I handle it alone, then. I go into town tomorrow, settle it myself. My own way. Then you got no more trouble."

"Concho—!" Nora screamed. "Stop it! Stop it!"

"He yo' husband, he my friend. I keep *my* promise, anyway."

Ramsey got up and faced Concho.

"All right, Concho," he said evenly. "You and I'll ride into town and see Sheriff Williams tomorrow. But we go unarmed, you understand? No guns, no knives, no anything."

"Sam, no!" Nora seized his arm. "It's not worth it! Hank's dead, we can't bring him back. You'll only ruin it here for yourself, for us—"

Ramsey covered her hand with his. "I made a promise, I'll keep it. Maybe Concho's right. Maybe if we don't go ahead and do it, Hank Stewart will haunt us for the rest of our lives."

Concho's face wore a broad, triumphant smile. Ramsey had taken Nora, and Concho would never get her back; but he was making sure that Ramsey paid the highest price possible for her; he would let Ramsey off from nothing.

Nora rubbed her face with her hand. "All right," she said finally, in a voice of weariness. "But if it's got to be done, I'll have my part in it, too. I'll go with you." Then she raised her head and looked at Concho. "And after that," she said in a voice full of ice, "you let me alone. You understand? *You let me alone!*"

Concho stepped back as if she had hit him. His expression did not change, but his color went as ashen as when he had been shot. "Sho, Miz Stewart," he said tersely. Then he turned on his heel. "I sleep in the barn tonight," he flung back and went out.

"Oh, Sam," Nora said in a grief-stricken voice, and Ramsey held her.

After the desert, North Wells seemed impossibly big and teeming. So many people, saddled horses, wagons, buckboards, parked automobiles . . . As the three of them rode in silence down the oiled main street and Ramsey was recognized, doorways and sidewalks filled with the curious.

Shan Williams was among them. As the trio reined in before the Sheriff's office, he was on the sidewalk, seersucker suit fresh, panama hat tilted back. He looked at them with the eyes of a hawk. "Hello, Sam. I never thought you'd come back."

"I did, though," Ramsey said, swinging down.

"Glad. Did you get your horses?"

"No," Ramsey said. "But the man who stole them is dead." Williams looked from him to Nora and Concho, still mounted. "Come in and tell me about it," he said.

"I've got a lot of things to tell you about," Ramsey said. He gestured. "Shan, this is Mrs. Hank Stewart and Concho Platt."

Williams swept off his hat and went around to help Nora down. "Glad to meet you, Mrs. Stewart," he said. "Y'all come inside . . ."

A half hour later, Shan Williams turned away from the telephone on his office wall and said, "Denning's on his way in. He's driving, so it shouldn't take over a half hour."

"Whut about the others?" Concho asked harshly.

Williams ignored him. He looked at Nora and Ramsey, who sat in chairs on the other side of his desk. Concho was on a bench across the little room. "I still can't believe it, though," Williams said. "That Tom Denning, Jim, Ralph, the others . . . To do somethin' like that and make no report of it to me when it was my badges they were wearin' . . ."

Ramsey said, "If you'd hanged an innocent man and let a woman to die in the desert, would you report it?"

"Maybe he wasn't innocent," Williams said. "I'm sorry, Mrs. Stewart, but—"

"If they'd thought he was a rustler," Ramsey cut in, "don't

122

you think they'da told you about it? The Mescans shot them up. They hadn't caught the cow-thieves. They had to take their mad out on somebody. Like Concho said, what about the others?"

"I'll deal with them in due time," Williams said. "But Denning organized this thing and led it—he's the one with the responsibility. We'll face him with it first."

"And then what happens?" Ramsey asked.

"That depends on Mrs. Stewart. If she signs a warrant for murder—"

"I'll sign it," Nora said in a dead voice.

"Then I'll arrest him—all of them . . ." Williams looked grim. "But, Sam, you're sure you know what you're doing? Arresting men like Denning and the others is one thing, getting them convicted is another. And if they're not convicted, you know what this county will be like toward you—"

"It's always been like that," Ramsey said.

"No," Williams answered. "It hasn't. You never could get it through your head, but that old grudge faded out long ago. The only ones who kept it alive were the antiques like Denning, some of the rest of the old-timers. Otherwise, the town don't give a damn about you one way or the other. You can be friends with it or enemies, the choice is yours. But you bring this against Denning and there won't be no questions. He'll turn this county against you harder than it ever went against your daddy."

"I can't help that," Ramsey said.

Williams stared at him a moment, then looked at the clock over Concho's head on the far wall. "All right," he said tiredly. "It'll be another twenty minutes before Tom gits here. Y'all go git some coffee and I'll call you when he comes."

They crossed the street to the cafe. Concho halted at its door. "You know they won't let me in," he said. "I'll hafta go down to Mex Town."

Ramsey said, "I'll bring you a cup out."

Concho spat into the dust of the gutter. "F'git it. I'll wait out here." He sat on the edge of the sidewalk.

"Concho," Nora said.

He did not look around.

"Concho, don't go anywhere else. I mean, not to a store. You promised me—"

"I know whut I promised. I ain't heeled. No hide-out gun, no knife, no anything—"

"Then don't leave."

"Ain't gonna buy one, if that's what worries you."

"It does," Nora said.

123

Ramsey took her arm, led her into the cafe. "He's clean," he said. "I searched him myself before we started out this morning."

Nora's face was pale. "I only hope so," she said. They sat down at a table. "Sam, I'm afraid."

"It's too late to be afraid now. Besides, you've met Williams. I told you he was straight."

"I know, but I can't help it. I've got the most terrible feeling—"

"It will all be according to law. The law will take care of everything."

"But Denning's such a big man . . ."

"Not bigger than Shan Williams," Ramsey said. "Not bigger than the law."

Nora smiled weakly and touched his hand. "Oh, Sam, you don't know people like I do. You've kept yourself apart from them all your life. But I . . . I've seen them at their worst. I know what they're like, how things work, what a man like Denning can do. It's the kind of trouble that can go on and on and—"

Ramsey thought of last night, of Nora in his arms, her body straining against his. He said, "No matter what happens, you'll be safe, I promise you that."

"Do you think it's me I'm worried about?"

Ramsey said, "Here comes the coffee. Drink it and you'll feel better."

They sipped the coffee in silence. Ramsey had just set down his empty cup when the telephone on the wall at the end of the room blurted three short rings. The counterman went to it. "Yeah," he said into the receiver, "I'll tell 'em." He hung up and turned. "Sam?"

"Yeah," Ramsey said.

"Sheriff Williams wants you. He says Tom Denning's in his office and for y'all to come on over."

When they went outside, Concho was leaning against the building, rolling a cigarette. He said thinly, "The big dawg jest drove up. He over there now."

"I know," Ramsey said. "Come on." He took Nora's arm and they crossed the street, with Concho trailing behind.

Tom Denning sat in one of the chairs across from Williams. He wore a Stetson, a neatly pressed but dusty suit, a tie. As they entered, he arose, pale-blue eyes playing over them, and swept off his hat. "Sam . . . This is Mrs. Stewart?"

"You know damn good and well who she is," Concho growled from behind them.

Denning's eyes flicked to him. "Ramsey, you better tell your black friend to sit down and shut up."

Concho took a step forward. Nora whirled and pressed a hand against his chest. "Concho, please!" He halted, then nodded, and went to the bench across the room. He sat down, legs crossed, lambent eyes trained on Denning.

Denning motioned Nora to his chair and sat on the corner of the sheriff's desk. "Now," he said to Ramsey, "before we git into the rest of this cock-and-bull story, I hear you killed Sheep Kelly."

"That's right," Ramsey said.

"Then you got a reward comin' to you from the Cattle Raiser's Association. I don't reckon you can produce the body."

"No," said Ramsey.

"Well, all the same, maybe I can help you get it."

"We'll talk about that later," Ramsey said. "Shan, have you told him?"

"He's told me," Denning snapped. "And I must say it's the biggest pile of damned foolishness I ever heard. We never killed no man named Hank Stewart. If he's dead, blame it on the Mescans."

"Why, you goddam liar!" Concho bellowed from across the room.

Denning whirled. "Nigger, you shut your mouth or I'll—"

"You see?" The cords stood out in Concho's neck. "You see?"

Nora's face was agonized. "Please, Concho—"

He fell silent, but his mouth was grim, his eyes smoldering, and they could hear the hoarse rasp of his breathing.

Ramsey said quietly, "You can tell it in court, Tom. We're swearing out a murder warrant against you."

"Booshwah," Denning said, but his face was pale. "You know so much, Ramsey, you see it happen?"

"No," Ramsey said. "But Mrs. Stewart did. You hanged her husband before her eyes. Concho"—he jerked his head —"saw it too."

"So that makes two witnesses." The color came back to Denning's face; he even smiled a little now, mockingly. "Two witnesses, against seventeen I kin call that'll swear it never happened. Shan, I told you this was a waste of time!"

Then Nora sprang to her feet. "I can't stand any more of this!" Her face was pale, but her eyes were blazing and her voice rang out forcefully. "Mr. Denning, you hanged my husband and I saw you do it! I saw you give the order for the horse to be whipped out from under him! I don't care how many witnesses you've got, how many lies you tell, nothing can change that—!"

Denning's smile vanished. Williams shoved back his chair. "Tom, you see how it is. I got no option but to put you under arrest. You can't laugh off a murder warrant when a man like Sam Ramsey will cosign it against you."

Denning turned his head, looking at all of them. Then, quite affably, he shrugged and held out his hands. "Sure, Shan. Put the irons on me if you want to. Don't worry, I understand—won't hold it against you. Like I said, I got seventeen witnesses against two, 'cause Ramsey says he didn't see it. And I ain't particularly worried about those two."

Ramsey said quietly, "What do you mean?"

That smile lifted Denning's mustache again. He dropped his hands. "What do you think I mean? Maybe there's something about these folks you don't know, Ramsey. When Stewart first moved into this county, I had the Association investigate him. And we found out some interestin' things about him, his wife and his black hand. I'm anxious to tell what I know to a jury and a judge about . . . Baton Rouge."

Sam Ramsey had become so accustomed to a gun that his hand went to his hip before he realized he wore none. Then a terrible animal cry filled the room. "You devil!" Concho roared, and he was off the bench like a panther. His huge body slammed into Denning, knocked him back across the desk, and then Ramsey saw the gleam of the knife Concho had pulled from deep in his boot. He brought it down, and Denning screamed and his legs threshed, and Concho struck with the knife again and straightened up and whirled as Denning's body slid to the floor.

"Noracita!" he cried in triumph. "Your husband's killer is dead!" And at that moment, Shan Williams shot him three times with a Colt automatic.

All three bullets caught Concho in the chest and threw him backwards. The knife dropped, and he sprawled against the bench, clawing at the wounds, his eyes suddenly big and round.

"Concho!" Nora cried, a sound of terrible grief. She ran to him, threw her arms about him, struggling to help him up.

He looked at her with those strange, round eyes. His thick lips twisted in an eerie grin. Then blood poured from his mouth and his body was dead weight, tearing itself from Nora's grasp, dropping heavily to the floor.

Nora stared down at it. A rasping sob broke from her and she turned blindly away. Ramsey was there to catch her in his arms.

126

"I thought you told me he wasn't armed," Shan Williams said, in a voice that shook with reaction.

"I searched him," Ramsey said. "So help me God. But it musta been all the way down inside that boot. He worked it out while we were in the cafe . . ." His voice was like iron. "It doesn't matter. If he hadn't done it, I'd have killed Denning myself, with my hands."

"And then I'd have had to shoot you," Williams said. He crouched over the body of Tom Denning, shook his head, and stood up. "All right," he said. "Denning for Stewart. Is that enough for you? Or do you want me to arrest the others."

Nora pulled away from Ramsey. "No," she said desperately. "No."

"You'd never convict them," Williams said thinly. He looked at Ramsey. "Let it lay here, Sam. Make your peace with the town. Tom was the guiding spirit in all this. The others were just followers."

Ramsey said, "But we've got to live here. And you heard about that report Denning got from the Association. Do you think—?"

"I think it was a confidential report to Tom," Williams said. "And I think that what was in it died forever, just a minute ago." Gently, he touched Denning's body with the toe of his boot. "If it didn't, if the others knew, they'll never dare breathe it, not as long as you don't bring 'em into court and force their hands. It can end here, Sam. Concho jumped Tom and I shot him. You've got a long way to go to build up your herd again. You're gonna need all the help you can get. Let it end here and make your peace with the town."

Ramsey looked down at Concho's sprawled body. He swallowed hard, full of grief and pity for this man who had been both enemy and friend, this man stronger than any he had ever known, strong enough even to endure the agony of the hopelessness of loving and being black. Nora was sobbing quietly against him. Ramsey thought: He knew all the time it would have to end this way.

Then, slowly, he nodded. "All right, Shan," he said. "It ends here."

"Good," Williams said. There was profound relief in his voice.

"I want the body sent out to my place. We'll bury him there."

"I'll see to it," Williams said. "Will you be there if I need you?"

"Not right away," Ramsey said.

Nora raised her tear-wet face and looked at him.

"First we're going to the mayor's office and get married," Ramsey said. "Nora and me."

"Sam——?" she said.

"We're not waiting any longer," he said. "My horses gone, Concho dead . . . we've both got to start all over. We're not going to lose any more time doing it."

"All right, Sam," she said, in a voice that was a choked mixture of joy and grief. She took out a handkerchief and began to dry her eyes.

A crowd had begun to form around the door of the sheriff's office. "We'll do that," Ramsey said, "and then we're going home." He took Nora's arm and led her to the door. The throng of people parted to let them by, staring at them curiously. As they crossed the street, Ramsey looked up and down it. Somehow the town seemed different, now that he was no longer alone.

★　★　★